D0090667

THE

LOST BOOKS

OF

THE ODYSSEY

THE

LOST BOOKS

OF

THE ODYSSEY

✦

ZACHARY MASON
"

FARRAR, STRAUS AND GIROUX

NEW YORK

S

Farrar, Straus and Giroux
18 West 18th Street, New York 10011

Distributed in Canada by D&M Publishers, Inc.
Printed in the United States of America
Originally published, in somewhat different form, in 2008
by Starcherone Books, New York
First Farrar, Straus and Giroux edition, 2010

Library of Congress Cataloging-in-Publication Data
Mason, Zachary, 1974–
    The lost books of the Odyssey / Zachary Mason.— 1st FSG ed.
        p.   cm.
    "Originally published in slightly different form in 2008 by Starcherone
Books."
    ISBN: 978-0-374-19215-0 (hardcover : alk. paper)
    1. Odysseus (Greek mythology)—Fiction.   I. Title.

PS3613.A8185L67 2010
813'.6—dc22

                                                        2009041810

Designed by Jonathan D. Lippincott

www.fsgbooks.com

3   5   7   9   10   8   6   4   2

Contents

CONTENTS

Preface

Despite its complexity, a handful of images are central to the *Odyssey*—black ships drawn up on a white beach, a cannibal ogre guarding a cave mouth, a man searching a trackless sea for a home that forgot him. Nearly three millennia ago a particular ordering of these images crystallized into the *Odyssey* as we know it, but before that the Homeric material was formless, fluid, its elements shuffled into new narratives like cards in a deck. Echoes of the other *Odyssey*s survive in Hellenistic friezes, on Cycladic funerary urns, and in a pre-Ptolemaic papyrus excavated from the desiccated rubbish mounds of Oxyrhynchus; this last contains forty-four concise variations on Odysseus's story that omit stock epic formulae in favor of honing a single trope or image down to an extreme of clarity. I hope that this translation reflects the haunted light of Homer's older islands, where the familiar characters are arranged in new tableaux, but soon become restless, mercurial—they turn their backs, forget their names, move on.

THE

LOST BOOKS

OF

THE ODYSSEY

A SAD REVELATION

Odysseus comes back to Ithaca in a little boat on a clear day. The familiarity of the east face of the island seems absurd—bemused, he runs a tricky rip current he has not thought about in fifteen years and lands by the mouth of a creek where he swam as a boy. All his impatience leaves him and he sits under an oak he remembers whose branches overhang the water, good for diving. Twenty years have gone by, he reflects, what are a few more minutes. An hour passes in silence and it occurs to him that he is tired and might as well go home, so he picks up his sword and walks toward his house, sure that whatever obstacles await will be minor compared to what he has been through.

The house looks much as it did when he left. He notices that the sheep byre's gate has been mended. A rivulet of smoke rises from the chimney. He steals lightly in, hand on sword, thinking how ridiculous it would be to come so far and lose everything in a moment of carelessness.

Within, Penelope is at her loom and an old man drowses by the fire. Odysseus stands in the doorway for a while before Penelope notices him and shrieks, dropping her shuttle and before she draws another breath running and embracing him, kissing him and wetting his cheeks with her tears. Welcome home, she says into his chest.

The man by the fire stands up looking possessive and pitifully concerned and in an intuitive flash Odysseus knows that this is her husband. The idea is absurd—the man is soft, grey and heavy, no hero and never was one, would not have lasted an hour in the blinding glare before the walls of Troy. He looks at Penelope to confirm his guess and notices how she has aged—her hips wider, her hair more grey than not, the skin around her eyes traced with fine wrinkles. Without the eyes of home-coming there is only an echo of her beauty. She steps back from him and traces a deep scar on his shoulder and her wonder and the old man's fear become a mirror—he realizes that with his blackened skin, tangled beard and body lean and hard from years of war he looks like a reaver, a revenant, a wolf of the sea.

Willfully composed, Penelope puts her hand on his shoulder and says that he is most welcome in his hall. Then her face collapses into tears and she says she did not think he was coming back, had been told he was dead these last eight years, had given up a long time ago, had waited as long as she could, longer than anyone thought was right.

He had spent the days of his exile imagining different homecoming scenarios but it had never occurred to him that she would just give up. The town deserted, his house overrun by violent suitors, Penelope dying, or dead and burned, but not this. "Such a long trip," he thinks, "and so many places I could have stayed along the way."

Then, mercifully, revelation comes. He realizes that this is not Penelope. This is not his hall. This is not Ithaca—what he sees before him is a vengeful illusion, the deception of some malevolent god. The real Ithaca is elsewhere, somewhere on the sea-roads, hidden. Giddy, Odysseus turns and flees the tormenting shadows.

2

THE OTHER ASSASSIN

In the Imperial Court of Agamemnon, the serene, the lofty, the disingenuous, the elect of every corner of the empire, there were three viziers, ten consuls, twenty generals, thirty admirals, fifty hierophants, a hundred assassins, eight hundred administrators of the second degree, two thousand administrators of the third and clerks, soldiers, courtesans, scholars, painters, musicians, beggars, larcenists, arsonists, stranglers, sycophants and hangers-on of no particular description beyond all number, all poised to do the bright, the serene, the etc. emperor's will. It so happened that in the twentieth year of his reign Agamemnon's noble brow clouded at the thought of a certain Odysseus, whom he felt was much too much renowned for cleverness, when both cleverness and renown he preferred to reserve for the throne. While it was true that this Odysseus had made certain contributions to a recent campaign, involving the feigned offering of a horse which had facilitated stealthy entry into an enemy city, this did not justify the infringement on the royal prerogatives, and in any case, the war had long since been brought to a satisfactory conclusion, so Agamemnon called for the clerk of Suicides, Temple Offerings, Investitures, Bankruptcy and Humane and Just Liquidation, and signed Odysseus's death warrant.

The clerk of Suicides etc. bowed and with due formality passed the document to the General who Holds Death in His Right Hand, who annotated it, stamped it, and passed it to the Viceroy of Domestic Matters Involving Mortality and so on through the many twists and turns of the bureaucracy, through the hands of spymasters, career criminals, blind assassins, mendacious clerics and finally to the lower ranks of advisors who had been promoted to responsibility for their dedication and competence (rare qualities given their low wages and the contempt with which they were treated by their well-connected or nobly born superiors), one of whom noted it was a death order of high priority and without reading it assigned it to that master of battle and frequent servant of the throne, Odysseus.

A messenger came to Ithaca and gave Odysseus his orders. Odysseus read them, his face closed, and thanked the messenger, commenting that the intended victim was in for a surprise, and that he was morally certain no problems would arise on his end.

On the eight succeeding days Odysseus sent the following messages to the court as protocol required:

"I am within a day's sail of his island."

"I walk among people who know him and his habits."

"I am within ten miles of his house."

"Five miles."

"One."

"I am at his gate."

"The full moon is reflected in the silver mirror over his bed. The silence is perfect but for his breathing."

"I am standing over his bed holding a razor flecked with his blood. Before the cut he looked into my face and swore to slay the man who ordered his death. I think that as a whispering shade he will do no harm."

3

THE STRANGER

I should have dreamed that night, of choking up a white bird that fought free of my throat, shook itself and flew away, leaving me empty and retching. But in fact there was no warning and I had no dreams, waking before dawn to a morning like every other morning on the long shore of Troy, alone in my tent—the smell of wood smoke, the light of false dawn, the silhouettes of passing soldiers on the canvas wall.

A hoarse voice outside my tent whispered, "Odysseus, son of Laertes, son of Autolykos, an enemy begs a word." I knew how easy it was to penetrate an enemy camp, having done so myself on many occasions, and I had given the Trojans much cause to hate me, so I stood and quietly drew my sword from its sheath. There was a genuine entreaty in his voice so I said, "Enter and have your word, enemy."

An unarmed man let himself into my tent. He looked simultaneously comfortable, surprised and as though he were exerting himself not to look over his shoulder. He muttered a quiet prayer to Pallas Athena which was un-usual in so far as she hates the Trojans and it was evident from my visitor's narrow features and dark hair that he was of that race and city. He said, "I bring you a host-gift, Lord. A riddle—thus:

"One: When I was a boy visiting my grandfather, a man of great will but widely despised, he told me that his father's father had counted both bears and men among his kin, this in the days before the red-hairs came. Though the blood is running thin, he said, the change still sometimes comes. He took me to a glade in a dark wood, drew a dagger with a wavy blade and cut deep into his wrists. I thought he was killing himself before my eyes and was going to run for help but fur erupted from his wounds and surged over his arms. His hands became padded paws with yellow half-moon claws and his irises turned mirror-green. The change stopped there and he soon reverted to the shape of a man,* exhausted and dis-satisfied. He said that an uncle of his had had the true power but as a young man had gone off to live alone in the mountains and never come back, even to visit. And

---

*Tales of lycanthropy are common among the Pelasgians, the pre-Aryan inhabi-tants of Greece. Their version of the disease was a sort of royal malady, far from benign but a certain sign of divine descent and the right to rule. The reference to the self-cutting with the knife is obscure—possibly it has to do with the mystery cults whose celebrants were said to be able to pierce their skins but shed no blood. Another interpretation is that the grandfather is cutting away his humanity to reveal the animal within.

this is the reason, he added, that our family is disliked and respected, though these days few remember it.

"Two: I went hunting with my cousins when I was just shy of manhood. I fell behind the hunt and, distracted for a moment, did not hear the boar coming. I raised my spear and tried to thrust but my arms had lost their strength and it gored me. My cousins came bursting out of the wood and killed it but I had already fallen. It was my first wound and I wept openly, from pain and surprise and because I thought it had unmanned me, though as it turned out the gash didn't extend beyond the top of my thigh.

"Three: There is an Olympian who loves me. The first time she spoke to me I was lost in the fog in the channel off of Zakynthos.

"Who am I?"

I replied, "You must be none other than that famous Odysseus, king of Ithaca, which is to say myself, for all these things happened to me, though I have never spoken of any of them. Did some god spy on me and whisper my secrets in your ear? Speak quickly, stranger."

He had been watching my face intently. Closing his eyes, he said in a dead voice, "I am not making game of you and if any god did this it was without my knowledge or consent. For I too am Odysseus, king of Ithaca, and the night before last I fell asleep on that bed and the next morning woke up in a house in Troy, as you see me now, one of them. With a new wife and new children, who call me Iapetus." He sat down heavily on my camp chair. "I feigned madness to buy time and hide my confusion. Tonight I slipped out of their city to see who was in my tent—it was strange to walk so carelessly past the Trojan guards. I must admit, you were the last person I expected to find here. I had thought it would be Iapetus the Trojan, or some stranger, and was ready to bargain, or kill him if he was going to disgrace my name."

"Your approach to assassination has the virtue of originality." I put my blade to his throat, ready for him to make a move. I have interrogated men at sword's point before—often I have seen in their eyes a conviction that they, heroes, cannot die under such ignominious circumstances and a nascent intent to turn the tables on me. At such times I stick them in the big artery in the neck, the same stroke I used to kill pigs in the slaughter-house back home (it is a quiet death, life coursing gently away over a few minutes, pleasant compared to some). "Say I am in Ithaca and want to move my bed into the great hall. What then? Answer quickly, or I will send you back to Troy." If the wind happens to blow your ashes that way, I added privately.

"The bed is built around an olive tree that emerges from the floor and passes out through the ceiling. I built it myself, starting work the day after my wedding," he said, opening his eyes. "The second day I smashed my thumb with a hammer."

"What was I thinking during the rain before last winter's great sally on Troy?"

"I was watching the young men dress for battle and thinking of my own son Telemachus, who is nearly old enough for arms."

I lowered my sword. The stranger looked miserable. Absently, he pulled out the water jar I kept under my bed and drank.

"What now?" he asked. "I see that my life is occupied. I made no plan for this. I cannot imagine a plan. In effect, I am exiled from my life. I wish I had not come."

Self-pity wearies me. "Here is what now. I have my life and you have yours, though it is new to you. I will continue to fight for Agamemnon, the fool, whose vanity has filled a thousand men's mouths with dust. You do what you want. You do not have my rights and are not bound by my oaths. Go and fight for Troy if you please— you know our counsels, could break our lines and bring the war to a quick conclusion," I said, hope rising within me.

He shook his head. "I have killed too many Trojans to change sides. And though I could slaughter the Greeks and win fame I would be a traitor in my heart. No. And I cannot join the Greeks and be a nameless turncoat. I take my leave of Troy today. I will find some place where

I can carve out a holding with my sword, some baron's daughter to marry."

I gave him a sack of food, another of gold, and arms and armor that I had stripped from a dead Trojan hero. He thanked me politely but seemed eager to go. I wished him well and told him that of the two of us I thought that he, freed from necessity, was the happier.

In due course, Troy fell and was sacked and the streets and the altars were strewn with dead. I had much honor and my pick of the spoils. Among other treasures I came away with a pretty slave-girl named Irina who had served in Iapetus's house. I overheard her talking to the other girls about a time years ago when her then master had lost his mind. He had developed a strange accent and would not look at his wife or children. For several weeks he had forsworn his usual companions and pastimes and spent his days walking the battlements looking out at the Greeks. One day he had come home at first light carrying a sack of gold and some armor that had once belonged to Sarpedon, who had died in battle. That afternoon he had taken a few men and all of his gold and gone away for good. The strangest thing, Irina said, was just before he left when she had walked in on him cutting his own thigh with a dagger—he looked like a sculptor, getting the cut just so. I was preoccupied with preparations for the trip home and spared only a moment to pity the victims of so-called Iapetus's stratagems.

After many years and travails I came to Ithaca's shore, full of caution. All my men were drowned, my ships sunk and my treasures scattered on the sea floor. I was ready for any sort of treachery or decay but found the kingdom to all appearances in good order. The roads were mended, the peasants cheerful and many tall ships spread white sails in the harbor. I asked a sailor who was king here and he said that Odysseus was king in Ithaca, of course. I went to my family's stronghold and introduced myself to the castellan as a wandering soldier and singer, looking for a place but not for too long—I had heard that Ithaca was prosperous and thought I would try my luck. I was courteously led into the great hall and there was Penelope, aged but still beautiful, and sitting next to her on my own seat was Iapetus the Trojan, bearded and sun-browned but still an alien, a foreigner, not a thing like me. Penelope's hand rested on his. Telemachus sat in the wings, watching me with polite hauteur. The king, the so-called Odysseus, stood and under his short tunic I saw a white scar on his thigh exactly where the boar had gored me. He said, "Welcome, stranger. Though you introduce yourself with humble speech, your bearing impresses me—you are obviously a man of the best blood and have the air of a captain. Indeed, you seem as though you might have been a king once. Sadly, times are peaceful and there is not so much call for courage as when I was young—I need no more men-at-arms, and have harpers enough. However, you will not go away without a meal, a bag of gold and a suit of armor. Speak highly of me and of Ithaca as fortune bears you elsewhere. Sometimes my mind will go with you as I tend to my duty here—of the two of us I think that you, freed from necessity, are the happier."

4

GUEST FRIEND

Alcinous, king of Phaeacia, and Odysseus, the wanderer, the eloquent, the silver-tongued, walked along wooded paths over high sea cliffs affording glimpses of the harbor, the distant city and the shining white-capped waves, the sort of place of which a man lost in mazy sea ways and the malice of petty gods might dream. Alcinous said:

> Among the Phaeacians it is believed that each man lives out his life as a character in a story told by someone else. The family and city of each person's storyteller (or possibly tellers) are unknown and perhaps unknowable but are subjects of frequent speculation. Certain philosophers are of the opinion that the evolution of history can be made to reveal the raconteurs' national character. It has come to be more or less widely accepted (on the basis of the irregular depredations of locusts, of the propensity of Phaeacian kings for taking black-

haired wives with green eyes and short tempers, of our excellence in archery, of the frequency in dreams of cavernous palaces carved into the living stone of low round mountains) that the storytellers are natives either of Phrygia, Sogdiana or distant Bamiyan. We have sent messengers to these kingdoms and even those beyond them but all have found nothing. The one thing on which all Phaeacians agree is that not enough is known to infer even a single teller's name.

Odysseus replied:

Wise king of the happiest country I have seen, is it not better to live your well-favored life never knowing the teller's name? As long as he is remote, a distant voice, an abstraction, you are the master of your life and lands and all things are possible to you. But once you have seen his face and taken his measure, then the endless possibilities, always an illusion, will dissolve, and your life will be revealed as the poor invention of a limited mind, rarely inspired.

And what if on seeing your kingdom, beautiful beyond compare, he were satisfied and fell silent? Perhaps it would be enough for him to end with a golden island in a distant ocean where a king and a storm-tossed mariner take the evening air.

Alcinous looked out over the ocean and said:

When his story ends a Phaeacian does not die but goes on to play another role in a different story told by the same teller. In this way the changes of station endemic to Phaeacian life are explained. Everyone in that city has a royal ancestor no less than four generations back and considers himself a prince biding his time—likewise, everyone has a great-aunt or great-uncle who must be confined in an attic.

Moreover, loyalties shift in Phaeacia as rapidly as the tide and there is a well-worn track from the throne room to the oubliette. Death finally comes, usually in the evening, when something in the raconteur fades out for good and in the midst of his story his eyes fix on the horizon and he trails off into silence, thinking of nothing. For this reason the Phaeacians consider silence an act of kindness, as sacred as guest friendship, a grant of repose to a distant stranger.

Odysseus looked at the man on his left and replied:

If you welcome death you are gently mad.

The path forked—fields and rivers lay to the left, and to the right, where Alcinous led them, were orchards and woods over sea cliffs. Alcinous said:

Death is unimportant. Even with the sweetness of the evening, the harbor full of my ships, the firelight in the palace windows, I would have lived enough, would have understood my life's shape, if I could meet the teller and know him.

And for all the failures of my agents in distant lands, hope is not altogether dead. Certain sages contend that in the oceanic vastness of time the sea will bring him to our shores.

Evening had come to Phaeacia, and though they could still see light on the water and the crushed white shells of the path they had themselves become indistinct, a pair of silhouettes deep in conference in blue twilight shadows. They came to an apple orchard where fireflies winked amid branches that groaned in the wind and Odysseus said:

Let me tell you a story, Majesty. On a remote island a king who shares your ambition walks along a path of crushed shells with a grey-eyed vagabond plucked from the sea. The vagabond is well spoken and full of ready invention—the king wonders whether this is the teller he has longed to meet. As evening settles, island and ocean become indistinct—ships become as waves, towers as cliffs and trees as ghosts. The amiable pair come to an orchard, already half shrouded in darkness. The wanderer, who beneath his bland and cultured demeanor has a mind full of rapine and whose name has been on the lips of innumerable noblemen as their mouths filled with blood, falls a few steps behind the sovereign, maintaining a constant flow of words to comfort and distract, for he sees bright arrowheads winking among the apple trees and hears the creak of slowly drawn bow-strings. He had been expecting the king to try to confirm his suspicions and now the means are clear: Archers lie in wait for the pair with orders to kill their king's companion—if he was the teller, he would not die in his own story and would thereby be revealed. And if he was just a man, well, no one need know that a nameless greybeard far from home died by treachery.

Odysseus paused. The gloaming had deepened and the orchard shook in a gusting wind that made his footsteps inaudible. When the wind subsided he went on:

Hark to the rush of the bird's wings, Majesty, so close around us. They say the gods send us messages in their flight.

To continue. The wanderer, whatever else he may be, is economical of means. He falls silent for a moment and moves to the king's left. As they come around a bend in the road the archers see their two shadows and fire at the one on their left who, though they do not know it, is their master, who I find has fallen behind me now, perhaps distracted by the humming passage of night birds, and now I am leaving the orchard alone as night swallows the last of the sun and I tell this story to myself, very quietly.

5

AGAMEMNON AND THE WORD

Agamemnon wanted a fortress on the wide plain before the walls of Troy but there was nothing to build with but a few trees and an unlimited quantity of sand. Therefore (at Odysseus's suggestion) the Greeks dug the negative image of a palace in the white plain, a convoluted warren where cascades of fine grains trickled endlessly down the walls and into the tenuous corridors irregularly shored up with masonry. It was an uncomfortable home but Agamemnon said two things of his new capital: that it was not fully in keeping with the dignity of his ancestors but was perhaps fitting for a king at war, and that if he failed to take Troy at least his tomb was built around him.

In the center of the palace Agamemnon sat in state on a throne of granite in a chamber supported by the ribs of a scuttled ship. Around him were generals, astrologers, sages, polymaths, priests and oneiromancers, all filling his ears with their murmuring. In this way the court functioned much as it had in Mycenae, except for the frequent cave-ins and sand-slides that suddenly obliterated rooms, courtiers, armories, armorers, elegists and exits. Following the wisdom of the court geomancers it was considered impious to exhume any of the collapsed rooms and tunnels, a sin on a par with looting a tomb, so when more space was needed the miners struck out into virgin ground. Thus the underground palace evolved dendritically, sending off new shoots in all directions, sometimes opposed by unforeseen aquifers or plumes of hard rock, working around these obstacles with ant-like tenacity.

One night a black cloud of grief descended on Agamemnon and he fell to brooding on the apparent perfection of his ignorance, exemplified by his failure to capture a single city in years of siege though he had ten times as many men as his enemy and god-like heroes ran to do his bidding. The failure of his knowledge, he reflected, extended beyond military strategy and encompassed all the world, even unto the names of his servants, the topography of his palace and the history of the blade hanging at his side. He called together his wisest men, Nestor, Palamedes and wily Odysseus, and commissioned them to write for him a book that clearly and explicitly explained everything under the sun, even unto all the mysteries hidden within the earth, the true names of every living thing, the number of grains of sand on the Troad, the secret histories of the gods and the tumultuous futures of the stars, all to be writ fair in no more and no less than a thousand pages.

The counselors conferred in low voices out of the king's hearing, speaking of the state of the king's mind and vanity, the innate interest of the task, whether the taskmaster would be able to recognize a solution, and finally whether their combined lifetimes would suffice to write the required book. At last they turned to the throne, bowed as one, and said it would be done. That night they left Troy followed by scribes and cartloads of gold, promising to return no later than as soon as they got back.

When they returned the king's beard had turned silver and his limbs were twisted like oak branches. The palace was deeper than when the sages had left—as floods and settling sands buried the first layer of tunnels new ones were excavated in the higher strata and the remnants of the old levels were relegated to storage, dungeon and thief-road. As for Troy, at nightfall bonfires smoked and crackled atop its towers and when the moon was full the sounds of a night market drifted down from its walls. From the roof of Agamemnon's palace the marketers' sapphire and emerald lanterns could be discerned, bobbing like distant fireflies in a wind that brought the scents of cardamom and cinnamon.

The three sages bowed before their sovereign and with a flourish presented a heavy book bound in tarnished silver containing a thousand thick, densely written pages. When opened the book released a waft like hot iron in a winter forge. Within Agamemnon read of many things:

The history of his ancestors the Atreides.

The detailed plans of the castle on the highest peak of Mount Olympus, and what dolorous event will transpire there on the day the engines of the world shudder, hesitate and begin their slow deceleration.

The mathematics underlying the populations of herring in the sea, the evolution of the stars and the fencing style of a certain little-known sect of Sicilian masters, and how these disparate things are secretly ruled by a single idea.

A survey of the many layers of the Earth and the currents and tidal schedules of its vast seas of magma.

A lexicon of the hidden language of cities, in which buildings are nouns, the inhabitants verbs, and empty spaces adjectives in an endlessly changing narrative.

A certain General Sun's theory of warfare, based on modern scientific principles.

The gossip and scurrilous propensities of every whole number from zero up to the largest number that had yet been conceived of by men.

. . . and a great many more topics besides. It had been impossible to fit this wealth of knowledge into a mere thousand pages (even with letters no larger than a grain of the ubiquitous white sand) so the sages had made the book read differently and coherently forward and backward, from bottom to top and top to bottom, if every other word was skipped, and if every third letter was ignored and so on.

Agamemnon read until his eyelids were heavy and his chin sank onto his breast. He gave a start, lifted his head and closed the book with a click. The sages silently awaited their due.

"This is not it. This is not it at all," said the king. "I wanted a book that gave me some understanding, not this cabinet of wonders and analogies, this encyclopedia of encyclopedias tricked into a millennium of pages. I am very disappointed. However. I will not punish you for your failure, in part because I see in your faces that you truly thought you had done well, and anyway, I have no wiser counselors to hand. So I will give you another chance, and this time I will make my orders exceedingly simple. Find the sentence, the single sentence, that contains the sum total of all wisdom." The sages bowed and withdrew, leaving the palace with caskets of jewels and companies of armed men.

They were gone for a very long time. When they returned, Troy had been abandoned, its moss-stained walls as worn as mountain-sides, the rusting hulks of war machines decaying on its parapets amid the tatterdemalion shells of factories. The levels of the Greek palace had multiplied, gone deeper—now it resembled a vast inverted castle, its battlements and towers soaring into the depths of the earth. Now and then a district was separated by a landslide and till the miners could reconnect them to the king's rule they lived with their own laws and minted their own coins. The years had turned Agamemnon hard and bright, scouring away everything patient and human in him. Palamedes, who exceeded even Odysseus in seeing into the inner workings of things, approached Agamemnon and presented him with a dagger sheathed in a red cloth. The king drew the mirror-bright double-edged blade and on both sides read, "And this, too, shall pass."

For a long time the king thought deeply and seemed almost to smile. "This is better. Here is a comfort in sorrow and a check on joy. But . . . even this is not enough. I have left too much room for interpretation and error, so I will rephrase the task one final time. Bring me everything, the skies and their clouds and the rain pouring into the oceans and every grain of sand on all the beaches, every ant crawling on a stone and every god in his pomposity, all in a single word." Showing no surprise, the counselors dispersed yet again. This time each went a different way from Troy and took nothing but the robes on their backs.

Seasons came and went with unseemly haste and in time Odysseus returned alone. Troy was a memory and the palace a kind of madness to which cartographers were susceptible. Odysseus took the king's skeletal bone-colored claw and slipped onto it a silver ring set with a blue gem the color of the western sky in the failing of the day. "Look into the gem, sire. There is your word."

Agamemnon looked but what he made of the word is not recorded because moments later he slumped forward, the interminable tyrant finally dead. Also not recorded is whether Odysseus had poisoned the ring or whether he had found the word and it sufficed.

6

PENELOPE'S ELEGY

Odysseus set foot on Ithaca trembling with wrath, his spear poised to fly through the heart of the first man unwise enough to cross him. He passed unopposed up to his old hall where instead of enemies he found his kinsmen turning to face him with wide eyes, exclaiming in wonder—he first thought it was a war-cry and nearly slew them. They drew him in among them, touching and praising him, all astonishment and delight except for Penelope (whose face had been the ground for the figure of his dreams), hardly aged and oddly quiet, lingering alone at the back of the crowd. He pushed his way through to her and reached out to touch her cheek but she evaded him and the crowd looked away, suddenly quiet, and Odysseus was aware that he had blundered. The next day they showed him her grave. For the rest of his time on Ithaca Odysseus avoided looking at her as she lingered in his house, staring out the window and idly running her fingertips over familiar things. He mastered

his desire to seize her legs and kiss her thighs and hands
for he knew she would turn to ash and shadow as soon as
he touched her and moreover nothing is more disgraceful
than to acknowledge the presence of the dead.

BACCHAE

When the Trojan shore sank below the horizon I
thought about what to do next. There was a sentiment
that we should go straight back to Ithaca but I decided
we would take the long way back and turn raider till we
saw our own harbor—we had a fleet of five ships, every
man was lean and hard from years of war and, taken by
surprise, the yeoman militias of the coastal cities stood no
chance against us.

We attacked at night, by preference. We put many
towns to the torch, speared men in night-dress fumbling
for their bows and filled our holds with stolen silver. We
struck and sailed on, trying to stay ahead of our reputation, but nothing travels faster than bad news and the day
came when we saw grim armed men patrolling the walls
of the city we had chosen. We could barely have fit
another tripod aboard anyway, so it was time to sail for
home.

It was nearly winter then, the tag end of the sailing
season, and flocculent grey fogs covered the sea. We

could easily have found an island somewhere, someplace out of the way, unlikely to be visited, and spent the winter there fishing and letting idleness smooth off our keen edges, but we were tired of our own society and of our rootless wartime existences and so we did not wait. We would have preferred to sail within sight of land but were afraid of well-armed ships cruising for revenge so we took the straight route over open sea. There was many an old sailor in my crew and none of them had ever made a blue-water crossing of the Middle Sea but I scorned adversity and risked it.

The days crept by, undifferentiated durations of mist and whitecaps. We kept course as best we could by dead reckoning but the sun and moon rarely peeked out—when they did my mates and I would jump on the opportunity and make our measurements but our calculations were never in agreement. Three ships went missing one night and were not to be found however much we called into the whiteness but it was no great matter, I thought, they could find their own way home.

On the seventh day of the journey the look-out shouted (his disembodied voice floating down from the fog-enveloped crow's nest) that he saw orange lights floating above us close ahead, too far up to be a ship. The fog shifted and we saw them from the deck, bright flares drifting high above us. It was hard to be certain if it was the cloud bank or the lights that were moving. The more superstitious men invoked the Hermes of Travelers and made the sign against the evil eye. I noticed that the lights were spaced evenly and seemed roughly rectangular and told the men to cheer up because we were looking either at the windows of a house on a high island hill or at some unusually symmetric ghosts. Within minutes we found the shore, steep and rocky and covered with short twisted pines. There was a cove and in it a neat little dock. It occurred to me to pass it by—we had treasure enough and supplies to get us home even if we wandered until spring, so why go looking for trouble? But with the impending reality of homecoming and the reversion from warriors to the conditions of husbands, sons and towns-men, the crew were determined to have a holiday. Re-luctantly I permitted them to dock and followed as they jumped from the ships, swords in hand.

The island was small but very steep, really just a small mountain protruding from the sea, its flanks covered with a dripping tangle of redolent pines. A single path zig-zagged upward, its stairs cut in the stone and lit by paper lanterns spaced out like stepping-stones so that on reach-ing a new one the glow of the next was just visible through the fog. Up we hiked, full of uncertainty. At the top we emerged into a clearing before a house with a high roof and an open door. Evenly spaced windows glowed with firelight. As we looked around doubtfully, moved by the house's beauty and unsure if we were pirates, pilgrims or travelers passing by, the lady of the house emerged and from her doorway greeted us with a warmth and composure that were shocking in light of the savage spectacle we must have presented. In retrospect, that should have been a warning. She said that we were welcome on her island, Aiaia—she and her women rarely received visitors and would gladly offer us their poor hospitality. Abashed, the men sheathed their weapons with pantomimes of discretion and entered her hall, meek under her magisterial smile. The lady's maids emerged to take our hands and seat us at a long table before a fire burning in a great pit large enough to roast ten bulls. Above the pit was a mantel carved with men chasing wolves or perhaps being chased by them. I wondered about the extravagance with firewood but thought it impolite to ask.

The lady, who said her name was Circe, sat me at her right hand and said that we were clearly heroes returning from some great struggle, she could see it in our keen faces and the strength of our sword-arms, and I had the air of a captain about me. Who were we, then, and what deeds had we done? This was against the law of hosts—guests were to be allowed to eat and drink before they were asked to account for themselves, but she and her maids had a wanton look about them and I suspected they were prostitutes as much as gentlewomen so I did not stand on politesse. I gave her a not entirely accurate history of the war, distorted more for the sake of a good story than self-servingly. I glossed Helen's death and said little of Agamemnon and his brother. I did let slip that I was the favorite of a goddess and that my counsel had often been sought by chiefs. She was an excellent audience, thoroughly enjoying the tale and prompting me to continue when I was afraid I had talked too much and fell silent.

It got late and the fire burned low. Many amphorae lolled on the ground, empty of wine, ringing hollow when someone tripped on them. The women started trickling away with my men, who took care to avoid my eyes as they went off to their forest trysts. (I don't know why—I never gave them cause to think of me as a moral exemplar.) Outside, torches went past the windows and the wind brought laughter. When everyone else had gone, Circe stood and took my hand and led me into her bedroom as the coals settled.

I woke later that night not knowing why but troubled and then it came again, a thin high keening. My first thought was that there had been a fight over a woman. I sat up in her bed and listened. I heard the wind in the pines, the distant waves, something like laughter and then a barely audible retching. Circe turned and muttered in her sleep. I crept out of bed and went to the window that opened over the mountain. Flashes of torchlight shone here and there among the trees. I watched for a long time, breath steaming and goose bumps rising. The sky was lightening in the east and I was about to go back to bed when I heard a long familiar ululation close by and saw a flash of bare skin through the restless boughs. This could have many meanings, some of them benign—in Athens the cult of the Bacchantes was an excuse for faintly licentious outdoor revels for well-to-do ladies. Then a woman walked naked out of the woods, her skin white and her tangled black hair whipped by the wind. Her face was blank and in her left hand there was a skinning knife. There were dark stains on her hands and stomach.

I drew my sword and put it to Circe's neck, the tip moving with her pulse. She came slowly to her senses and regarded me with sleepy, slitted eyes as I stood menacing her. In a husky voice she told me to think—if she had wanted me to die she would have drugged me like the rest of my men, all of whom were gone by now. She said she desired me and had decided to keep me, called on my dispassionate mind and held out her hand for the blade.

They were only women and probably had no better armament than knives—even alone, I could cut my way through them, and there might even be a few of my boys left alive. It occurred to me then to wonder what they had done with the unguarded ship. I imagined stalking down the path with blade drawn, racing onto the dock unopposed and finding nothing there but the waves lapping at the pilings as lights flared in the house high above me. I imagined coming back up to the house, finding it empty, searching for a target for my rage, finding nothing. The sun going down again and distant wavering cries calling and answering from the forest. It horrified me that I should have made it through Troy, often avoiding death by the width of a spear blade, only to end up dying here, my bones turning to ash in her fireplace.

A way out will present itself, I thought, as I handed her the hilt. There was no hurry. She gestured for me to come back in beside her and I did. She whispered in my ear that she was sure we would be happy together for a long time and that I would be understanding when she had new guests.

8

ACHILLES AND DEATH

When he was drunk Achilles would take his knife and try to pierce his hand or, if he was very drunk, his heart, and thereby were the delicate blades of many daggers broken. Odysseus, who had seen more than one such demonstration, rained praise on him for his extraordinary mettle, which made Achilles bridle like a puppy, but privately worried that a man immune to death must soon despise the mortals around him. Certainly Achilles thought little enough of the Trojans. Odysseus had seen him emerge from battle bristling with black arrows—as he undressed to bathe the shafts came away with his armor and he would loll in his bronze tub while Briseis* washed his unscathed limbs and Patroclus told jokes.

Wounds fascinated Achilles. When Patroclus got a scratch Achilles would fuss over him like an old nurse, endlessly bandaging and salving what could as well be left alone. But when a Greek was mortally wounded, even

---

*A slave girl, the captive of his spear, of whom Achilles was fond.

one of his own men, Achilles would not so much as look at him. When the bodies of the fallen were wound in orange sheets and burned on a pyre, Achilles was always elsewhere.

On the field Achilles was haggard with rage, to all appearances pursuing a vendetta, as though the Trojans had plotted to steal his cattle or his standing. His style was uninformed by tactics or consequences. A high wave surging onto shore, breaking over a dune and washing the sand away in a foaming tumult—so it was when Achilles struck an enemy line. Odysseus often trailed behind him to pick off the wounded and terrified.

Odysseus noticed that although Achilles was indifferent to blows, he received very few, apparently because his enemies were too dismayed to attack him intelligently. Odysseus considered imitating him but decided that the enabling recklessness had to be deeply felt. He did, however, make a mental note to be cautious of men with nothing to lose.

Achilles barely suffered the presence of King Agamemnon—he would talk over him in council and walk past him in camp without so much as a nod. With uncharacteristic self-possession, Agamemnon put up with it, perhaps because it was not clear how he could retaliate. The aristocracy joined Agamemnon in hating Achilles but the rank and file loved him—when the mood took him he would beggar himself in generosity, giving away his gold and spears and slaves to some warrior whose smile he liked or who had done a brave thing in battle.

One night when innumerable watch fires burned on the Trojan wall, Odysseus was summoned to Agamemnon's tent. There he found the High King with Nestor and Menelaus speaking darkly over a single candle. Nestor pulled Odysseus close and whispered that Achilles, only half drunk, had been talking mutiny, strutting around camp and proclaiming that he was nearer a god than a man and it was unseemly that a mere contemptible mortal should command him, especially when that mortal could not even take one city in seven years' siege. His Myrmidons laughed and encouraged him. Agamemnon said that while Achilles was a terror to his enemies, he was nevertheless more boy than man and any enterprise of his which did not hinge on his sword-arm would end in disaster.

The discussion turned to the method of Achilles' dissolution. Though he was proof against weapons and no one had ever known him to get sick, he could, they reasoned, be bound. He could be tricked into a mine and buried in a deep shaft under heavy stones where only bats would hear him calling. He could be immersed in molten iron and wrought into an ingot to be dropped into the sea, there to spend eternity listing in deep currents. He could be locked into a heavy chest and hidden in a secret compartment in a trader's ship, itinerant, anonymous and never seen again. But besides the innate difficulty of inflicting these schemes on a man who was fearless, invulnerable and an exuberant killer surrounded by loyal and heavily armed friends, there was his mother, Thetis, a sea nymph who loved her son dearly and had the ear of Zeus the cloud-gatherer, who saw everything. Odysseus reflected on the problem for a while and told them not to worry, he would take care of everything.

Three nights later he went into Achilles' tent in the small hours and crouched by his cot. "Achilles, wake up. I'm setting an ambush for the Trojans by the Scamander and I need you," he whispered. Achilles shrugged off sleep and, laughing at Father Odysseus's sudden boldness, buckled on his armor.

They went silently over the white starlit plains to a hive-shaped tomb on a hill over the river. The tomb's door was open. Achilles reluctantly followed Odysseus into the low cool earthy room where pale bodies lay wrapped in flame-colored cloth, from which Achilles averted his eyes. "Wait here," Odysseus said, "I will call like an owl when they're coming." "I will go with you," said Achilles. Odysseus said, "No. You can break men but lack subtlety. I will go hide and watch and when the time comes for killing, then you join me." Achilles' eyes glowed like a cat's in the faint light as Odysseus shut the tomb's door and barred it behind him.

In high good humor, Odysseus walked into the hills to the camp he had prepared. For three days he stared out to sea and drank in the silence. On the third night he left his tent and returned to the tomb. Pausing in front of the tomb's door, he envisioned pursuing spearmen—his breath quickened and he started to sweat. Unbarring the door, he said, "Achilles! Forgive me—I was taken unawares and only tonight managed to escape, I think," and peered fearfully over his shoulder. He had composed a story in which he had been captured but made the Trojans think that he was a wanderer who had come to Troy to loot the battlefield dead. He had concocted a detailed description of the notional patrol that caught him and even a back-story for his character as a looter. These preparations proved unnecessary. Within the tomb Achilles sat with his eyes closed, concentrating on each slow, shuddering breath.

The next morning Odysseus told Agamemnon that Achilles had gone away, having concluded in the course of his imprisonment that he should alleviate suffering rather than cause it. This explanation was deemed suspect but Achilles' absence, sorely felt, was a certainty.

Subsequently it was said that he had gone away into the East and become an ascetic or a sophist. Over the years stories trickled in, most of them hardly credible: Achilles had begged in the streets, preached to animals in the waste or spent a year in contemplation in the shadow of a tree. The Greeks neither credited these travelers' tales nor thought that they diminished his lingering glory.

9

ONE KINDNESS

Odysseus clung to his raft of sticks as he was washed through the breakers and onto the shore of another island in the sequence of islands that filled his days. On the narrow shore the cold rain hit him and he found himself missing the warmth of the sea. He saw firelight in a cave, pulled himself up and staggered toward it. It occurred to him to walk in and throw himself on the mercy of the occupants but instead he thought, "One more time," and crept through the freezing, rain-soaked night to listen.

Within, three women sat around a snapping fire. The shadows on the wall behind them were the blurred silhouettes of sweet maiden, stout matron and bent crone, but as the firelight flickered the shadows took other forms—a long-armed ogre with grasping hands, a bird of prey with unfurled wings, a net with glass floats (their iridescence gleaming on the rough rock walls), or, sometimes, nothing at all. They debated loudly to be heard over the rain and the fire, which, for all the violence of its burning, made more smoke than light.

"Ten years is ten years, no matter how you cut it," said one, brandishing a cooking knife. "You can interpret all you like but the facts are inescapable."

"Mere simple-minded literalism," said another, using a ladle to stir a tarnished copper pot on a tripod all but swallowed by the flames. "If it said he was to be brave like an eagle, would you have him plucking mice out of fields and climbing a tall tree to sit on a nest of sticks and guard an egg? It is understood to be a guideline, an indication to be fleshed out as required by the details of the situation, and not an exact recipe . . ."

"It is exactly a recipe, only far more binding," said the first in a voice like a fast, cold wind.

". . . unless you're a blockhead," finished the second.

"Blockhead yourself, Miss I-shall-do-as-I-please-for-it-is-only-a-guideline," said the first. "I beg your pardon most humbly, great Madam. I never meant to imply that one as august as yourself should be obliged to be bound by the iron chains of necessity."

"Tut. There is some room to move within those chains, and I say he has suffered enough," replied the second.

"He has not begun to suffer," said the third, whom Odysseus now saw was the fairest and most terrible. "If he got home now he would be unmarked. His suffering, as you are pleased to call it, would be the stuff of tales to enliven the winter of his old age, stories for his grandchildren. Fie on you. We will draw him thin and fine."

It began to hail. The ice stones clamored in the trees and off the stone and the cave filled with echoes.

"Bloodthirsty," said one, he could no longer tell which.

"Then let none of his blood be spilled. We can hurt him just as much, even worse without it," said another, cackling, her voice coming from no direction and every direction.

"What then, break his heart?" said another.

"Don't break him—drain him. Take all his warmth and hope and make him empty as a clear cold night on the top of Aetna."

"So be it."

"So be it."

"What next for him, then?"

"The witch Calypso, in solitude on her island. Her bed is cold and she longs for him, though she does not yet know it, for all that she studies the stars and suspects that the sea will soon bring her a gift."

"And shall we make her a horror?"

The hail crescendoed and the fire was a red glow of embers. Odysseus gathered his courage (thinking that after all the shadows might only be shadows, the women only women) and in a high, rough voice said, "No, let her be beautiful and as kind as summer."

"Such kindliness, sister!" said one.

"Not from me," said another.

"Never mind, and so be it," said the last. "We have

other business to transact. There is death to be dealt in Hyperborea."

"But do not forget," said one, as the fire disappeared altogether and the women merged into the shadows, "he is, for all that he is bound by us, allowed just once to direct his fate, though I for one shall not seek his counsel. Let us hope he does not meddle enough to get himself home."

10

FUGITIVE

The high fires on the Trojan shore illuminated the revels of the Greeks, their long shadows writhing behind them. Their ships rode low in the water, heavy with gold and slaves, and their adversaries were in chains or in hell. Odysseus, architect of the victory, watched his comrades stagger triumphantly and lent half an ear to the crying of gulls, hoping to hear Athena. Agamemnon, mouth purple and scabbard flapping emptily, found him and asked why he sat off by himself, to which Odysseus replied that ten years had accustomed him to vigilance. Agamemnon said that the dead would not be arming themselves and if they did, the Greeks had beaten the very gods, so come and drink to our victory over the Trojans, the dogs, and may nothing grow in their broken, salt-sown city but weeds and evil rumors. Odysseus said, "The house of Priam is broken, his sons dead. There is nothing left for you to curse." Agamemnon stood with great dignity, adjusted his breast plate (an ill-fitting treasure looted from the battlefield), and went away.

That night Odysseus dreamt of the ruins and saw the gods rebuilding the city's shattered wall. Next to him Athena leaned on her spear and watched the work. Odysseus asked why the gods were rebuilding Troy, when some of them, even she, had been at such pains to destroy it. "The gods are not rebuilding Troy," she said, "as it has not yet been erected." "Then what are they doing?" asked Odysseus, pointing. She turned her head, recognized him and said, "You should not be here. Run away quick!" Her fear chilled him. Just then the last stone was laid on the city wall; its gates swung open silently and came to with a click.

The next morning the men pushed the grey ships down the beaches into the green sea. As they sailed away the camp's cold fire pits and abandoned barricades looked as forlorn as Troy's black husk.

Odysseus's homeward trip, first joyful, soon became a misery. Fate seemed to have a grudge against him and his Ithacans, sending them in quick succession the cannibal cyclops, the lotus eaters, the sirens, Circe, and inexorable Scylla. A year stripped Odysseus of all his men (gone down to death) and all his ships (torn to flinders or sunk in the sea) and found him clinging to a crude raft as he drifted alone through a bad sea.

Odysseus woke as the water closed over him and thrashed his way to the surface, crying out, though there was no one to hear him. The fog was thick—there was nothing to see but whitecaps and sticks from his raft that sank as he snatched at them. There was no better strategy than striking out hard for land—for all he knew, he would find it. There was not much hope, but it was better than waiting to drown, so he started swimming. He regretted that there were no landmarks and he was, possibly, swimming in circles. His shoulders burned and then his lungs and he was nearly spent when, to his amazement, he drove his hand into something hard that resonated under the blow. He looked up and saw faces peering down at him from a grey ship with a long eye on its prow.

A familiar voice said, "I expected better from you, if only a better escape." Strong hands pulled him up and dropped him on deck. He lay there thinking that whatever circumstance he had stumbled into, it was bliss to draw breath, feel the ship moving under him and not think of drowning. His eyes were blurry with salt but, rubbing them, he found himself looking at Agamemnon's golden greaves. "Did you think you could desert so easily, after I went to so much trouble to recruit you?* Can this be Odysseus of labyrinthine mind?"

The sailors, embarrassed on his behalf, avoided looking at Odysseus. He put on dry clothes and realized they had been brought by Alkanor, who had died with a Tro-

---

*Odysseus did not want to leave Ithaca to flight at Troy, so he feigned madness in hopes that Agamemnon would go away. Palamedes defeated his ruse by threatening the infant Telemachus with a sword—Odysseus moved to defend his son and thereby revealed his rationality.

jan arrow in his heart the day of Hector's funeral. The fog was gone, the sun hung in the sky, his heart beat. There was nothing to say.

Agamemnon had the unresisting Odysseus locked belowdecks. After sleeping, he searched the hold and, finding nothing, broke into Agamemnon's cabin (its lock was contemptible). Among weapons, wine cups and trophies of war he found a book called the *Iliad*. It was the tale of his war and the gist was right but the details were often wrong. In the introduction he read:

> It is not widely understood that the epics attributed to Homer were in fact written by the gods before the Trojan war—these divine books are the archetypes of that war rather than its history. In fact, there have been innumerable Trojan wars, each played out according to an evolving aesthetic, each representing a fresh attempt at bringing the terror of battle into line with the lucidity of the authorial intent. Inevitably, each particular war is a distortion of its antecedent, an image in a warped hall of mirrors.
>
> The *Iliad* and the *Odyssey* have sometimes, through authorial and managerial oversights, become available to their protagonists. Surprisingly, this has had no impact on the action or the outcome. Agamemnon is too obstinate to change his mind and anyway never believes what he reads.

Achilles flips through the *Iliad* and shrugs. Priam makes sacrifices to the nonplussed gods and anyway thinks that he is above prophecy (recall Cassandra). Perhaps there were once characters who read the book with dawning apprehension and fled that very hour, finding refuge in the hills, never again to meddle in the affairs of cities and gods, but if ever there were they are long gone now.

In time they came to Troy and there was Achilles, bright as gold and full of life, leaping from his ship's prow, the first to set foot on Asian soil. The Ithacans arrived and gathered around Odysseus, asking him where he had gone and why he had left his own ship and taken a berth with Agamemnon. He had liked most and mourned all. They asked him what moved him so—it had been just two weeks since they last had seen him. Odysseus said he had seen by signs and portents that it would be a long war.

Everything fell out as before. In the first year Achilles fought a Trojan champion who was proof against blades and stones and strangled him with his helmet strap. In the second year Hector led an attack on the Greek camp and killed Agamemnon's younger son. In the third year the Amazons fought alongside the Trojans and slaughtered many Greeks with javelins. And so on—as though choreographed, the Greeks attacked the city and arrows and death found their appointed marks. Odysseus knew who was going to die, so he was able to say his goodbyes. Men said he was bad luck.

He saw Athena from time to time, though she was silent. Sometimes she looked at him with pity. Other times her face was unreadable.

He looked at his image in polished blades and water. He could have been a battle-hardened forty or a weathered twenty. He thought of stealing a ship or wading into the sea with stones in his pockets, but for his men's sake he stayed, even though he thought they were illusions, or a dream.

The time came for him to steal into the city and see Helen. They spoke as they had before and as he knew they must. He had forgotten most of their conversation so he improvised. He thought he saw recognition in her eyes, and, as he left, their hands touched, a novelty.

In due time he proposed the ruse of the horse. He sat in its belly listening to the Trojans debate whether to burn it or push it into the sea, to Cassandra's weeping, to Priam ordering it brought within the city walls. That night he and his men crept out of the horse, opened the gates and set fire to the city. By midnight his face was black and his sword-arm was red to the elbow. He saw fallen enemies die again, heard old screams again, saw a tower he had burned to ashes risen in flame. In the palace he found Helen brushing her hair. Without looking away from her mirror she told him that ten years ago she had been dragged back to Menelaus's house and thrown into their old bedroom as half a wife and half a slave. The next morning she opened the door to a tap-tapping and there was Paris,* her lover, long dead and turned to ashes and now shyly beckoning. Helen hid her golden hair under Odysseus's hood and that hour they fled the city and went out of Troy's history.

In a fisherman's hut Odysseus held her and told her about the book. He supposed they would have ten years, then they would see. Athena never spoke to him again.

---

*Helen's husband and kidnapper, the instigator of the Trojan War.

11

A NIGHT IN THE WOODS

We forget ourselves in company. When I led my men into the Trojan ranks or through haunted unmapped islands I wore a dauntless mask, neither smiling nor frowning, always taking the next step, whether toward flanking the enemy's archers or improvising a sail from our ruined stores or getting us back to the ship just ahead of our pursuers. The essence of that mask was pride—my men loved me not for being right but for my intransigence, instant decisions and intolerance of any slight. It made me a monster of ego, which was wearisome, but while they were in my charge I had no choice.

Now it has been years since I have been lost at sea and they have been lost for good. With no uncertain young faces looking to me I have become contemplative, used to thinking things through in my own good time. And so, as the Phoenician ship touches at Ithaca I neither weep nor throw myself onto the shingle to kiss my native ground. Instead of dressing myself in finery and going to my old hall with arms open and a foolish smile on my

face, I put on a worn old brown cloak and sling a peddler's pack over my shoulder, the better to have a quiet
look around. Penelope is more than an ordinary woman
but many outrages can happen in twenty years. Still, I am
prepared to forgive—all that matters to me is that my
house is strong and, above all, that Telemachus, my son,
flourishes. As I walk away up the beach and the wind fills
the Phoenician's sails the captain shouts goodbye in his
strange patois and promises to call again in a month's
time.

I go through the forest to the old highway and head
toward town with my eyes open. Peasants and merchants
walk past, ignoring me. They look well fed but keep
their eyes on the road. I come to town and see smoke rising from every chimney and houses in good repair,
whitewashed and clean. It is, however, very quiet—no
doors slamming, mothers calling or children shrieking.
My conviction that all is not well is cemented at the
fountain, where the women get their water and stride
quickly home without so much as passing the time of
day. I sit down on the low wall of a corral to think about
my people, who have become as timid as the knot of cattle lowing nervously behind me.

I am reminded of the village of my father-in-law
Autolykos.* Nevertheless, I collect myself and as it gets
dark go toward what was once my hall, guided by the red

---

*The name Autolykos is usually translated "The Wolf Himself."

torchlight glowing from its high windows. With the ham of my fist I pound on the gate—"Open up, good people! It is Nohbdy the peddler come to deal—let me in and show me some hospitality!" The door is opened by a greasy young man with a glazed expression. His bearing suggests breeding but he barely acknowledges me, gesturing at me to follow him down the hall with a loose flick of his wrist.

We pass through the clean-swept courtyard, where cracked bones are piled against the walls. I shape my face into a mask combining greed and cringing humility and prepare myself for what I now know I will find in the great hall. On my throne Penelope lounges, taller than I remember, her presence filling the room. Young gentlemen orbit around her with vacant faces and deferential postures, lighting up when she notices them. There is no furniture except the throne and piles of matted furs strewn on the ground. It smells musky, like an animal's den.

Penelope toys with the black hair of a lanky young man who lounges at her feet, his arm entangled in her legs, and studies me balefully while the men study her. She orders a maid to bring me meat and wine, and as I eat I say, "I have news that you will rejoice to hear, dread queen. Not a day's journey behind me is Odysseus Laertides himself, your husband and king, returned alive after many years of suffering. His Lordship did me the honor of speaking with me and entrusted me with a message for you—he says that the first thing he intends to do upon getting home is move his bed out of the bedroom for airing. That was all of his message, and I swear to you every word is true, or I am not Nohbdy."

Penelope sniffs the air and smiles toothily, thanking me for my welcome but—and here she almost purrs—extremely surprising news. She regrets that her house is full tonight—I should come back tomorrow and there will be room enough. The black-haired boy, apparently a favorite, pipes up that they have no other guests, so why can't the peddler stay, but she puts a finger to his lips. Though her movements are gentle there is a new predatory light in her eyes. As she surreptitiously sizes up the men who crowd around her, their stupid, trusting, Ithacan faces remind me of my own men, all lost, and I make a hasty goodbye, leaving sooner than is polite.

I set off into the warm night, walking briskly, not minding much where I am going so long as I put the hall out of earshot behind me. After many miles I find an abandoned shepherd's hut, just visible from the road. I try to sleep but end up lying under my cloak for hours listening to the crickets play and the wind sigh through the branches. Every time a branch cracks I bolt upright, poised, alert, sword in my hand, holding my breath. Probably just foxes making their nocturnal rounds. I know I am being absurd. I think of Penelope's green eyes and the mooncalf faces of her lovers. I wonder if I performed the rites properly and my men, all dead now, have such peace as the shadow kingdom can afford. I wonder how Telemachus is doing and wish I could have seen him. By the time the moon sets I have given up on sleep and go outside to sit on the porch and stare out into the dark woods.

While I wait for dawn, my mind turns back to the one time I met my father-in-law Autolykos, lord of high peaks and deep valleys a week's hard journey into the mountains of the mainland. Wolf song had ushered me up through the last pass and into his domain, a prosperous quiet land where the dark pines were thick up to the edges of the fields. I was picking my way along a narrow track in a dense stretch of forest when he stepped out of the trees with his daughter at his side and greeted me. A young deer, just gutted, was slung over his shoulders. He was a rangy, wild-looking man with the quiet air of one who had never been contradicted. His daughter, Penelope, was barefoot and wore a torn, ill-fitting dress that hung so awkwardly she might have just shrugged it on. There were twigs in her hair and she never smiled but even in her bare, muddy feet she walked with a careless hauteur that would have discomfited Helen. Autolykos led me through his village and down to the deep river valley where his hall was built, an old place, mostly underground, with the roots of ancient, still-living trees for pillars and a foundation. The servant was clumsy, singeing the venison and burning his fingers. As we ate, Autolykos made odd little formal stabs at conversation.

We discussed the weather (unseasonably cold for spring), the wheat (which seemed to bore him), the wars in the East (of which he knew nothing) and the migration of elk (which, finally, engaged him). He and his silent daughter ate with their hands. He watched me sidelong as I used my knife. Ithaca is not so cosmopolitan and it was the first time I had ever felt effetely civilized.

When we had washed our hands he questioned me about my family: Who was my father? My father's father? How long had my line been kings? (He suppressed a snort when I told him five generations.) Were there heroes among them? Was there any madness, divine possession or shameful defect of person? Then he interrogated me about my island: What were the forests like? Was the hunting good? Was it far away from every other place where men lived? How well could I control my people? I painted a portrait of a line of kings who had been at the periphery of the great events of Hellas but had never permitted the slightest infringement of their prerogatives or weakening of their bloodline, and of a harsh island of many valleys, full of mists, favored by hunters, where it was easy to lose one's way. Of the people I said they were strong-minded and though the land was poor they were not—Ithacans were steadfast, good fighters and better traders. He asked about the character of the people, their religious observances and what they feared. I sensed he was circling around something and replied that in Ithaca people minded their own business and that in any event if I chose to give them a queen they would not only accept her but like it too. This seemed to satisfy him. He drew me up and embraced me, wishing me good luck and long life, large dominion and many children, and said that he would be gone in the morning. He smelled sharp and musky, full of spices. Then he showed me to my room, comfortable but practically a cave, and that was the last I ever saw of him.

I slept deeply that night, for all that the forest was full of movement. Sometime in the small hours Penelope came in to get me, clad only in her shift, her eyes green in the moonlight. She shook me awake and led me by the hand out into the woods. I assumed that it would be futile to ask for explanations. We went deep into the forest and all I could see in the sighing darkness were stray patches of moonlight on the pine needles.

She pulled her hand away and vanished. Entirely awake, I balanced on the balls of my feet, listening, hands out as though to feel currents in the air. I could hear motion among the trees, now here, now there. I saw a flash of green eyes. Something moved behind me and I ducked as she sprang at me, the fur on her flank brushing my shoulder. My eyes had adjusted and I caught just a glimpse of her, and she was a fine thing, so very fleet. She didn't lunge again but stood in a patch of moonlight where I could see her face, where amusement and threat were written in equal measure, but I showed no fear and she disappeared again, coming back moments later, a

woman again, and insinuated herself into my arms. Hera*
was never invoked and there were neither gifts nor priests
but I suppose that was when we were married.

The next day I led her out through the valley and up
through the mountains and soon after we sailed for
Ithaca. I brought her to my father's house and she was
gracious with her new relatives but privately complained
that the place smelled like centuries of dead wood and
men, though I think that really she was just homesick. To
please her, I built a new house, centered around our bedroom, in which I carved our bed out of the wood of a
wide-trunked, still-living olive tree, its fruits falling onto
our roof each summer. She did not want it said that she
was strange or that she clung to the old ways, so we kept
the bed a secret, even from the servants.

The next morning I take my armor from my pack and
cast away Nohbdy's cloak and name. I find a stream and
shave with my dagger. I stride into town in the center of
the road, very much the master. There are no guards at
the gates but a maid sees me coming and flutters inside.
In the empty, newly white-washed courtyard another
maid is weeping hysterically, surrounded by three others,
one of whom is gripping her shoulder and speaking to
her in a low, brutal whisper. They see me and fall silent,
their faces blank. I go into the great hall and there is

---

*Hera, the wife of Zeus and goddess of marriage, was always invoked at weddings.

Penelope, a head shorter than me, green-eyed and pretty in her red dress, smiling demurely. She embraces me and says all that is right and sheds a tear of happiness as the maids energetically scrub the already pristine flagstones behind her. One maid hurries past us on her way to the midden with a sack of scraps from the slaughter-room. The cloth sack is soaked through and a second maid runs behind her to wipe up the trail of red droplets.

The celebration lasts into the night and our reunion is entirely convivial. I tell Penelope about the war and my many exploits, already feeling myself becoming a bore whose only conversation is of battles long past. She seems not to notice when I skim over Circe and Calypso, and for my part I take no notice when her own history becomes light on detail. In the evening Telemachus appears, back from hunting, and greets me respectfully. I kiss him and turn his face this way and that in the light, pleased beyond words to see him.

Ithaca Town gradually comes back to life. There are a few squires inquiring into the whereabouts of their fools of sons, gone missing, and dour farmers impertinent enough to bring me dark insinuations, but they are quickly dealt with and soon there is peace. Almost overnight I cease to be the clear-eyed wanderer and undoer of men and become, as my circumstances require, the level-headed lord of a small island, settling disputes about sheep and planning with my engineer to dredge the harbor. Penelope is attentive and I am happy to be back with her, though of course I would not tolerate the slightest insubordination, let alone infidelity.

Telemachus is an excellent young man. He can throw a javelin farther even than Achilles could and outruns his peers without breaking a sweat. He is affectionate, loyal and fiercely protective of his house. In him, the preeminence of my house and line are secure for generations, though for all my satisfaction it sometimes gives me pause to see he has his mother's eyes.

12

DECREMENT

In the lassitude after love Odysseus asks Circe, "What is the way to the land of the dead?"

Circe answers, "You are muffled in folds of heavy fabric. You close your eyes against the rough cloth and though you struggle to free yourself you can barely move. With much thrashing and writhing, you manage to throw off a layer, but find that not only is there another one beyond it, but that the weight bearing you down has scarcely decreased. With dauntless spirit you continue to struggle. By infinitesimal degrees, the load becomes lighter and your confinement less. At last, you push away a piece of coarse, heavy cloth and, relieved, feel that it was the last one. As it falls away, you realize you have been fighting through years. You open your eyes."

1 3

EPIPHANY

I mutilated his son, the cyclops,* but he had outraged the laws of hospitality that bind both gods and men and Poseidon knew it. The waters were calm when I sailed away from that island, my spear still caked with the clotted humors of Polyphemus's ruined eye. I needed a story, though, and the notional grudge of the sea lord was a plausible one—people are willing to attribute any amount of ill-tempered vindictiveness to the gods. Even after she forsook me I was unwilling to embarrass her.

She carried me through the war. Nestor said he had never seen a god so openly love a mortal, and I suppose it is true. So much so, in fact, that my friendships with other men were strained—more than once I overheard someone call me uncanny, and some of the Achaeans made the sign against the evil eye when I passed. But I

---

*There was a race of cyclopes but one of them, Polyphemus, was the son of the sea god Poseidon. In the traditional version of the *Odyssey*, Odysseus blinds Polyphemus and thereby incurs Poseidon's hatred.

did not care—their fear added to my mystique and made them pliable, easy to manipulate, and anyway I had her.

She spoke to me often, manifesting as a brother warrior, or in the cry of a seagull, or in the crash of waves, or very rarely as herself, a tall severe woman with a long thin face whose skin was so pale it seemed to glow. Our discussions were mostly concrete—she would tell me not to leave my tent that night, or to seek out a certain Trojan in the fray, or what lie to tell or inanity to feign to survive the next few hours. Now and then she would be talkative and tell me what she had seen in the wider world—giants grumbling and talking rebellion among the roots of mountains, a lightning-riddled storm cloud scudding over blood-warm equatorial seas.

Some nights when the fighting had been fierce I would open my eyes and, still half dreaming, see her standing over me in the moonlight, leaning on her spear, gazing into the distance and appearing to ignore me. Something in her indifference rang false and I knew she was watching me. She was like a cat who likes company but will not suffer herself to be touched. I never said anything but her presence was a comfort to me.

Sometimes her aid was direct—twice on the field I saw her from the corner of my eye coming in like a black cloud to envelop an enemy and cast him aside drained of life, emptied like a wineskin.

In time Hector died and was buried, Troy was sacked and then burned, Helen was in Menelaus's bed again and all of Priam's line were sent hurtling down to Hades. My ships rode low in the water with Troy's riches and the golden, god-forged armor of Achilles lay wrapped in scented linen in my cabin, treasure to reinforce the preeminence of the Laertides in Ithaca for three generations. The next morning we were to weigh anchor and all the men were ashore for a final carouse with the companions they would most likely not see again. I was aboard ship checking every cable, line and sail, to ensure that all was seaworthy after a decade aground on the beach. She was there with me, suddenly, and as always in her presence I saw the world in sharper relief. I wasn't unduly surprised to see her—perhaps there had been something in the voice of the wind that forewarned me. Usually she was armed, holding her spear with a soldier's ease, but this time she had no weapon and no armor. She had on a plain white dress and, disconcertingly, wore her hair down—she looked almost girlish. I had seen her brighter but never so warm. I was ashamed to find myself desiring her and violently quashed the impulse.

I remember her every word and every intonation. I will not repeat what she said, though it will always echo in my daydreams. The broad sense of it was that she was offering me everything. Which is to say, herself. And as the husband of an Olympian, and one of the greatest in strength and honor (as she quite correctly reminded me), I would be given immortality. We would have all eternity together. All would fear us and love us and no one could ever touch us.

I am old in killing and I do not always attack from the front. I have seen friends die before my eyes and trampled their bodies as the battle and the hot day wore on. My skin is thick but her embarrassment made my knees weak. She was blushing and ran too quickly through what was clearly a prepared speech, she who is never at a loss for words, never doubts or hesitates. This was Bright-Eyes, Grey-Spear, Battle-Lover and Quick-Thinker, whom I had seen run laughing to fight hand-to-hand with Ares, the render, contemptuously turning his spear-thrust and driving her riposte neatly through his shoulder. Warming to her oratory, she praised the depth of my understanding and the quickness of my mind, comparable only to hers even among immortals. She praised my beauty and my composure (the latter I am willing to grant—as for the former, I am strong enough but no dancer, neither tall nor smooth-skinned nor so young anymore). I felt like a child watching his father, incorruptible and immovable, beyond all weak human passion, dissolve into tears.

I need hardly add that I could not accept her. What would I do, be her Ganymede, fetching wine and beaming while she spoke with her equals, her pretty boy with scars, wrinkles and sun-black skin? Or, worse, I could master her, be a proper husband and make her my helpmeet and bed-mate, have her wait on me while I spoke with Father Zeus on kingly matters. The idea is absurd. Even if it could be otherwise, she is beautiful and quick and her mind is like a lightning flash but she is a god, and therefore remote, and I cannot imagine her as anything else. I started to compose an eloquent and humble demurral but to my lasting regret I could not keep from laughing. She flushed bright red and for a moment looked so furious that I thought I would die in that instant—the gods' affairs, failed or otherwise, rarely end well for their lovers.

But she did not strike me down. Her face cleared and she kissed me on the cheek, once, and vanished. I have not seen her since.

Not long after that things went bad. I do not think she persecuted me—that would be beneath her—but I have felt her absence, and I think no river nymph or wind god will risk her hatred to help me. And I was reckless, after she left me, and I paid for it with my ships, all sunk now, and my men, all dead now, with no tombs to mark their passing.

14

FRAGMENT

A single fragment is all that survives of the forty-fifth book of the *Odyssey*:

> Odysseus, finding that his reputation for trickery preceded him, started inventing histories for himself and disseminating them wherever he went. This had the intended effect of clouding perception and distorting expectation, making it easier for him to work as he was wont, and the unexpected effect that one of his lies became, with minor variations, the *Odyssey* of Homer.

15

THE MYRMIDON GOLEM

Wounded pride justifies kidnapping, Agamemnon thought, when the pride is mine. He had just recruited the magus Odysseus from Ithaca by holding a sword to his infant son's throat. He might have asked him to come but greatly feared the Trojans and dared not risk a rebuff. With characteristic self-assurance he assumed that his victim would soon accept his servitude as a fait accompli and embrace his, Agamemnon's, purpose. Odysseus hated him as much for his presumption as for the kidnapping. From the bow of the ship he watched Ithaca recede and longed for his workshop, where he could have summoned a cackling sylph to seize Agamemnon and maroon him on the iciest peaks of the Caucasus. In the event he saw no option but biding his time.

A week out of Ithaca the ship touched at Syros.* Odysseus was told to go recruit the warrior Achilles, and to do it within a day, or he, Agamemnon, would sail back

---

*An island in the Aegean Sea.

72

to the now unguarded shores of Ithaca—he always needed more slaves. Agamemnon said, "The oracle at Delphi decreed that Achilles must sail with me or I will find a bad death waiting when I come back from Troy. Of course you see why I chose you, of all my men, for this mission." Odysseus was amazed to see that Agamemnon expected him to be moved by his fulsomeness. Nonetheless, he disembarked and went to the court of the Syrian king Polyxenos, an old friend and a fellow devotee of the hermetic arts.

Polyxenos told Odysseus that Achilles, late his ward, had died, bitten on the heel by an adder. His mother, the sea nymph Thetis, had appeared in a cloud of grace and nursed him but the poison was implacable and on the seventh day the boy went down to Hades. Odysseus held his head in his hands—not even a sorcerer could call back the dead and Agamemnon was a resolute and stupid man who prided himself on being unmoved by reason.

Polyxenos took pity on his friend and suggested that they use their arts to fashion a clay simulacrum of Achilles. Such an imitation would not withstand close inspection but it could fool everyone for a while. If need be, the double could be discretely dissolved in the sea. He observed that no one in the Greek army had ever set eyes on Achilles—who were they to doubt the Achilles they were given? Objections sprang to Odysseus's mind but, as he had no better idea, he mastered himself and agreed with as much enthusiasm as he could muster.

In the small hours of the night the two lords crept out through the postern gate and filled canvas sacks with wet riverbank clay. By the time the moon set they were in the cool, dusty palace cellars, shaping the clay into a man. His proportions were heroic on the theory that idiosyncrasies are suspicious in an aristocrat but anything at all may be expected of a man whose very frame proclaims him half a god.

They lured a pretty young slave girl to the cellar with hints of assignation and preferment, and cut her throat as soon as she walked in the door. They hollowed out a cavity in the golem's chest and filled it with her blood so that the golem could partake of her bloom. At cockcrow the girl's body was buried under an oak tree and the golem was done down to the least hair. Odysseus carved the word "Life" into the prostrate thing's forehead and its dull eyes opened.

The golem's cheeks were flushed and his skin was as warm and smooth as newly fired porcelain. When he stood up he seemed to be jointless. Second thoughts swarmed in Odysseus's mind—the hair did not look real, the skin tone was wrong for a Mycenaean, and his gaze had a strange, intense fixity. It was too late to change anything, though, so they girded him in armor, put a spear in his hand and told him that his name was Achilles. The golem did all they bade him do, opening doors and putting away knives and alembics, but for all their commands and cajolery he would not speak. Odysseus would have turned the thing back to dust and started over but Polyxenos reminded him that the king was waiting. He summoned his son Patroclus and told him to go with Odysseus and help sustain the ruse. In the first hour of daylight they swathed the golem in black cloth and hurried him onto the waiting ship.

Agamemnon was delighted to have avoided a bitter fate. Odysseus and Patroclus quietly monopolized their charge, who, on the rare occasions when they were not with him, stood board-straight by the railing and stared at the horizon. Odysseus explained his reserve as the hauteur of one more god than man, and Patroclus explained it as homesickness. Eventually Odysseus admitted to Agamemnon that Achilles was somewhat unbalanced by divine influences and unlikely ever to resemble an ordinary man—he had not revealed it earlier for fear of being accused of failing in his task and dooming his wife to shackles. Agamemnon laughed and told him he need not worry about such quibbles when he was dealing with a great-hearted man of honor.

At Troy, Patroclus shared a tent with Achilles and it was widely assumed that they were lovers. In fact, Achilles was tireless, endlessly biddable and intelligent enough to cook, mend and polish, which allowed Patroclus to live in the indolent luxury he craved.

Achilles' eloquence in battle made up for his muteness and the ruse went undiscovered. Once Paris shot him in the face with an arrow at point-blank range—it stuck, quivering, in his cheek. Achilles pulled it out in a puff of dust, threw it away and went back to his bloody work. In the confusion of battle, with friend and foe besmirched with white earth and blood, he sometimes killed at random, ignoring the Greeks' terrified, indignant cries, and so he became feared by Greek and Trojan alike.

Odysseus approvingly surveyed the stacks of Greek and Trojan dead piled up by his creation—the Trojans were a lawful enemy and mere foreigners besides, and as for the Greeks they were fools serving a fool of a king.

His delight in the ruse ended when Hector put his spear through Patroclus's heart. Achilles saw Patroclus die and went to stand over the body, shooing Hector away and trying to rouse his dead friend. The Trojans circled warily—Achilles killed those who got too close. The battle moved away but Achilles stayed with the body through the day and the night, sometimes nudging Patroclus with his foot, sometimes looking around as though for help, but he was the only one left on the moonlit plain. On the morning of the second day some understanding of death must have seeped into his thick clay skull because without warning he snatched up a spear, ran half a mile toward the thick of the fighting and threw himself in headlong. He fought in a rage, killing Greek and Trojan indiscriminately. He ignored the cruelest blows and his arm never tired—the flower of both armies poured their blood onto the field and soon all fled, leaving Achilles standing listlessly among the bodies with a bronze sword dangling from his hand. He reversed the blade and thrust it at his abdomen, snapping it.

In the following days both sides kept to their strongholds and even then they were afraid Achilles would overwhelm them, indifferent as he was both to blows and to entreaty. Peering over their barricades, they saw him walking a slow circuit around the city wall, dragging Patroclus behind him by the heel, occasionally looking back to see if he was stirring.

The Greeks had had enough. Agamemnon fulminated but he could not stop them from breaking camp and taking to their ships. Odysseus was relieved that no one had thought to question him about Achilles' extraordinary behavior and decided it was time to bring an end to his creation's career. On a grey morning when the other captains were getting their ships ready for sea, he got a handful of black mud from the banks of the Scamander and went alone to the deserted plain where Achilles made his grisly circuit around Troy (it had been three hot days and Patroclus's remains were faring poorly). "You there! Come here," said Odysseus with a confidence he did not feel. "I am here to help. I will make your friend there as alive as you are." Achilles approached him, all innocence, his burden ploughing the dust behind him. "Give me your helmet," said Odysseus. As Achilles lifted it off, Odysseus reached up and smeared the mud on his forehead, effacing the word "Life." Achilles stood there holding his helmet in his hands, as still as any stone.

Odysseus reflected that he hated both sides equally and might as well do both a disservice, so he loaded the inert golem into a cart and drove it to the Trojan gates. To the guards on the walls he shouted, "Achilles, scourge of the plain, is no more—he went mad from grief and flung himself into the sea. He was our best man and we have no more stomach for war. Accept, then, this memento of our strife, a statue of him who was both our strength and our undoing. Take it, if you want it, and put it in your city to honor the man who slew your best but in the end preserved you." Odysseus walked quickly away as dark clouds rolled in, the rain fell and the mud ran down Achilles' face in black rivulets.

16

THREE ILIUMS

A long time ago someone unknown to me lay on this cooling stone under a fading sky and sensed more than saw the ragged herds of oryx and ibex moving slowly through the bush. The tension in the air grew as the sun sank and the torpid predators pricked up their ears in their trees and lairs, waiting for the plain to be immersed in their medium, the dusk. A lion in silhouette stretched her long spine on the peak of a lone hill overlooking a white beach and the sea, a defensible spot, a good place for a city.

A long time from now someone unknown to me will stand on the white plain where I now stand. He will speak a different language and the mountains in the distance may have been ground down but there are certain constants that will reliably inform his life—kings like great trees whose roots are watered in ignorance, men who come to war reluctantly only to discover they have the souls of jackals, and fortresses like mountains, as immovable and inevitable. I anticipate that a flash of intuition will make him look at the tumulus or crater or clamorous sprawling city where Troy once stood and intuit how many men once bent their minds toward its destruction.

These strangers used and will use their wits to understand the world as far as they are able, though that was and will not be very far, and they did not and will not know where they come from nor who they are. Their ignorance, I infer, also encompasses the true names of the stars, the language of birds, and the key to the circuitous and ever-present defences of Troy. How can it be that I, enjoying the greatest advantage, the only advantage, of living in the present, am just as ignorant?

17

SIRENS

Circe had told me that the sirens' song was irresistible, the very shape of desire, and that no one who heard it went unscathed, as was attested by the bones of their admirers tumbling back and forth in the tide-pools around their reef. But I have never been one to leave a riddle unsolved or, as I overheard my men say, well enough alone and I was determined to hear them for myself.

It seemed that my curiosity could be safely indulged through simple logistics. As the ship neared the sirens' rock I had myself bound to the mast while the crew stuffed their ears with beeswax. It seemed odd no one had thought of it before but in general there is no accounting for the bovine stupidity of mankind.

There were two of them. As we approached the white breakers around the reef I saw them sit up, stretch their long spines and fix us with their gazes. Their torsos were too long, their fingers had too many joints and their eyes were cold and green. One said something to the other in a high musical language and my eyes began to water—the other laughed and they began to sing.

As they sang I remembered the face of a Trojan whose name I never knew whom I had killed before the high walls of that city, the man's surprise as I attacked him blind-side, how easy it was to slip my point past his guard and run him through, the Trojan's dawning rage at the affront to his body, an emotion half formed on his face when death found him, the tug on my blade as his body fell away. I remembered the first time I saw Penelope, walking away from me in a white courtyard in Sparta. I remembered Ithaca the day I left it. I saw how far I was from home, how remote the chance I would ever see it again. The sirens beckoned, longing for me, offering release from my displacement, but I laughed with delight at being lost and reckless, wandering among unknown islands, not knowing the shape of my days. "This is not so bad," I said to myself. "Anyone unmanned by these monsters is a home-body or a sentimentalist."

The sirens, who had been watching me intently, fell silent, briefly nonplussed. They conferred in low voices and I thought they might have given up when they launched into a new song, an intricate counterpoint comprised of just a few themes, varied and interwoven.

Their song broke over me and it was as though a veil had been blown away. I saw how Achilles, whose humanity was subsumed in speed and strength and reck-less pride, had made his inevitable slow march toward

death, dragging Agamemnon and Patroclus and all the Greeks and the royal house of Troy stumbling behind him. I saw the implacable self-assertion of Agamemnon mirrored in pious, gentle Priam's refusal to save his city.*
I saw Hector's love of country and family opposed by Achilles' madness for glory and his slight impatience for the death he knew was closing in on him. And overlaying them all were the passions and rivalries of the bright gods, like scirocco winds scouring everything they touched. Finally I saw myself, how my wit exceeded that of other men but gave me no leverage against fate, and how in the time to come it would avail me nothing but possibly an understanding of the full scope of my helplessness.

As their song crescendoed I had the sudden conviction that the world, which I had considered the province of meaningless chances, a mad dance of atoms, was as orderly as the hexagons in the honeycombs I had just crushed into wax and that behind everything, from Helen's weaving to Circe's mountain to Scylla's death, was a subtle pattern, an order of the most compelling lucidity, but hidden from me, a code I could never crack.

Abruptly, the song ended and I sagged forward, the ropes digging into my chest as the men took the ship out. I cried out for the sirens to continue, that I was close to

---

*Presumably the author means that Priam could have saved his city by violating guest friendship and giving up Paris to the Achaeans.

an answer, but they watched me depart with their chins propped on their hands.

I tried to reconstruct their song while its echoes yet lingered in my mind but all I could remember were four lines:

Achaea's old soldiery
Charmed out of time we see.
No life on earth can be
Hid from our dreaming.*

When the reef was well behind us the men unbound me. Making an effort to appear self-possessed, I told them that I had not had time to hear quite all and that we must go back. The men looked at each other sidelong, shuffled their feet and avoided my gaze. I cursed them, called them disobedient dogs whose lot was to obey, not to question. Reluctantly, they did as I asked, replacing the wax in their ears, rebinding me to the mast and retracing our course. They anchored the ship within bowshot of the monsters and stood guard by the rail with arrows nocked and spears lowered.

The sirens regarded me and said nothing. They beckoned with their strange hands and smiled (I wondered how they managed not to cut their tongues with such

---

*This is identical to the text of the sirens' song from Book Twelve of the standard *Odyssey*.

long, sharp teeth). I pled with them, begged, fulminated. They might have been amused. Soon they lost interest and lay down to sleep on their beds of twisted black basalt. A nervous crewman released an arrow that clattered on the rocks before ploughing into the sea.

The men conferred among themselves by signs, then weighed anchor and took us away, leaving me bound to the mast. I bellowed at them to turn back but they ignored me or pointed to their ears with exaggerated incomprehension. We sailed at good speed all day and left the sirens far behind us.

They freed me by torchlight. An order was on my lips but I saw mutiny in their deliberately blank faces and went to sit in the back of the ship, looking out over the flat moonlit sea and thinking of the sirens sprawled languidly under the stars, arms entwined, singing quietly to themselves over the hissing of the waves.

18

THE ILIAD OF ODYSSEUS

I have often wondered whether all men are cowards like I am. Achaea's flower, the chosen of Ares, disciplined, hard-muscled men who do not know what fear is—all a fraud, a conceit for bards and braggarts that has nothing to do with the vapid squalor of war.

I have no talent for martial arts. I was the despair of the arms master but I was the heir and to his sorrow he was in no position to give up on me. When I dropped my practice sword, hit myself in the head with my spear or broke down in frustrated tears, he would smile grimly and with forced good cheer say, "*Anyone* can learn to fight with enough application." And, lo, the good man was right—despite my clumsiness, fat, stiff muscles and inclination to cry under stress I did eventually attain a modest standard of skill at arms, thanks mostly to my father watching our practices and encouraging the master to beat me bloody if I gave anything less than my absolute best. And beat me he did, and often, though to his credit I do not think he relished it. After a whipping he would help me up, dress my wounds and say, "Sorry, boy, but it's your father's orders and you'll get worse than that when you go to war." I dreamed of coming into my title and having him flogged and enslaved.

The exception to my general military ineptitude was with the bow, at which I excelled. When I pulled the string the world became quiet and I was aware only of the target, which I regarded with interest but no malice as my arrow all but invariably found its mark. Unfortunately for me this only exacerbated my reputation for effeminacy—as it allows one to strike from safety, the bow is a coward's weapon, the sort of thing used by nomads and Asiatics. I could shoot rooks in the eye at a hundred paces all I liked and still be despised.

My shameful aptitudes did not end with archery—I was also articulate. I have never been at a loss for a tale, lie or synonym. I could recite the epic of Hercules after hearing it just four times. I was ideally suited to be a bard, a profession fit only for villeins, wandering masterless men who live at the pleasure of their landed betters, as my father reminded me when I broached the idea. He and his men would say things like, "We are here to live the stories, not compose them!" Sing, Muses, of the wrath of godlike shit-for-brains, hereditary lord of the mighty Coprophagoi,* who skewered a number of other men with his pig-sticker and valued himself highly for so doing.

---

*Excrement eaters.

When I was twenty, Agamemnon the High King came to the island to raise an army. His brother's wife had preferred a sloe-eyed prince with a palace to her lawful husband, a Spartan king who lived in a mud hut and slept with his pigs for warmth. Privately, I saluted her common sense.

My father volunteered me to lead our troops. Age was slowing him down and he had lately been transferring more administrative responsibility to me but I hadn't expected to be war-leader so soon. I had been making a point of carrying myself as I thought a battle-hardened hero would, loudly scorning danger, and though I thought my act was transparent enough for a child to penetrate, it seems I had convinced both my father and the men in the guard—they gave a cheer when they got the news and immediately started divvying up old King Priam's daughters and treasures.

Refusing to go to war was impossible. The only excuse would be madness or infirmity, and it would have been very suspicious if I were struck by a terrible disease just when it was time to sail. At this point a man of the common run would have realized the situation was impossible and bowed to fate but my cowardice made me capable of the extraordinary.

My father threw a feast in the High King's honor and I got my first good look at him. I knew his reputation as a warrior but in his face was a willfulness such as I had never seen. He looked like a man who would lash out with all his strength if crossed even minutely.

I played the part of the young-buck-keen-to-make-a-name for all I was worth. How eager I was to leave boring, quiet Ithaca, see the world, win renown by feats of arms and so forth. Looking distant for a moment, I said, "And Troy is a long, long way away? If a man took ill there I suppose he would have no option but to stay and fight?" and darted a quick, inquisitive look at Agamemnon. Palamedes, Agamemnon's lieutenant, a bald, silent man who thought much and spoke little, looked at me as though I had suddenly become interesting.

After a few minutes I made myself look as ill as possible and made my excuses. I went out, closed the door behind me, and, taking a deep breath, fell down thrashing, my heel hammering against the floor. The door opened—there were Agamemnon and Laertes, Palamedes and the arms master, all the men I had grown up with looking down at me as I writhed on the ground, saliva dribbling down my chin. Through my convulsive chattering I growled, "Close the door. Close the door!" Abashed, they did, leaving me to complete my fit in private. After a minute I desisted, sick with relief.

The next morning I showed up for arms practice as usual, face ashen, very grave. Father was there, nearly unmanned with grief—his son was damaged goods, all but unmarriageable and not fit for battle. Agamemnon clapped an avuncular hand on my shoulder and asked me how I did, and Palamedes asked if I ever felt the touch of god when the fits came on me. I knew that seizures were often preceded by epiphanies, so I reluctantly admitted that I did—sometimes, I told them, it was as though Pallas Athena herself spoke with me while my spell played out, whispering secrets in my ear. It was the first thing that came to mind. I had their rapt attention, which made me confident and, like a fool, I embellished on my intimacy with the god. Agamemnon smiled and I was horrified to see in his face an emotion I had thought alien to him—generosity. "My boy, your luck is in. Palamedes here was telling me about the warrior Laon, who suffered the same disease you do, but it never slowed him down, not for a moment. So you see, there is no need to be concerned. And I'm even told it's lucky, the god's-touch disease. And for this campaign I believe we'll be needing all the luck we can get, ha ha!" He clapped me on the shoulder again and went off to see about his ships. Palamedes smiled at me before following him and I decided that if I got the chance I would kill him.

I had hoped that the war would be short and I could return with an undeserved reputation for bravery. Spirits were high, in the beginning. Agamemnon and his lieutenants expected a quick victory but it was soon evident to me that there would be no such thing. The Trojan walls were high and thick, our siege engines were grossly inadequate and there was not a single skilled sapper in the army. The Trojans were as aware of our weaknesses as we were ignorant of their strengths—they would only sally when they could bring overwhelming force to bear at little risk to themselves. Most of the time they were content to let us spend our strength against their impregnable walls.

Their city was larger and their fortifications stronger than anything in Achaea—I realized that Agamemnon was basing his strategy on his experience attacking the little towns on the Attic coast. I was the first, but by no means the last, to realize that our failure was certain. I tried to persuade Agamemnon and his cronies with artful words but they scorned me, wondering rhetorically which campaigns I had fought in and whether I wouldn't rather skulk off home, leaving honor unavenged and glory lying in the dust? In vain I argued that honor could as well be served without wasting time, men and matériel.

The camp smelled of unwashed men, which was bad enough, and made worse by drunk soldiers who couldn't stagger the hundred feet to the latrine trenches. Only I seemed to mind the stench—the others breathed it in as though it were perfume. They were content to spend every night drinking and lying about their conquests of cities and women. During the day they fought and those lucky enough to survive came back to camp to repeat the cycle the next day, world without end.

Many times I was on the verge of just leaving and sailing back to Ithaca. I did not flee only because I would have lost all face with my father and our subjects. As Father and I know, and as we try not to remind them, there is no good reason for our subjects to pay their taxes, row our ships, fight our battles or tip their caps to us other than tradition and the threat of violence (which is implicit, nicely civilized and glossed over in the older, better families like mine). Much as I loathed the war, there was at least the prospect of a tolerable life afterwards. My father would have disinherited me if I had shamed our house and I would rather have died than come down in the world.

I have speculated that brave men do not exist, but Achilles son of Peleus was an exception. The young chief of the Myrmidons was built like a mountain but fleet as the wind. Women found him comely but he reserved all his affections for two young men, Patroclus and Antilochus. In combat he was the most cold-blooded and terrifying man I have ever seen. I took to following in his wake on the field—I earned the first notches in my shield by finishing off the Trojans he wounded. Here, I thought, was a man who was in his way as different from the common run as me.

I made him my study. He was devoted to a sea goddess, Thetis, in front of whose portable shrine he sat for hours each day in silent prayer. I watched him train with Patroclus and the Myrmidons. He came to practice early and for every javelin his men threw, even the champions, he threw three. He was, in his way, as relentless as death. Cultivating him was easy, as the other chiefs found him stand-offish and abstemious and he had few friends. It was easy to draw him out—I got the sense that he liked to talk about himself but rarely got the chance. He told me he had been blessed by Thetis at birth and made immortal, immune to every weapon. But for all that, his immunity was limited—the day of his death was already fixed by Fate and not even the gods could change it. He therefore intended to win what glory he could in his set span of days. I questioned the value of an immortality that lasted exactly until one died but his fatalism was impregnable and he laughed at me and called me a sophist.

The war dragged on for years. Only our numbers kept us from being routed. We lost five men for each one of theirs, which was, alarmingly to my mind at least, considered an acceptable rate of attrition, as we outnumbered them ten to one. I did not wish to number myself among the sacrifices and therefore became a skilled tactician, anticipating the places where the Trojans would attack and being elsewhere. From time to time I would guess where the Trojans would be weak and ambush them, just to avoid getting a reputation as a man who avoided trouble. Over the years lines of tribal authority weakened and men with knowing eyes and similar dispositions gravitated to my troop.

I was with Achilles when his fate found him. Hector,

the mainstay of the Trojan army, had appeared in the thick of battle and scattered the Greeks. Achilles went straight to meet him but his bodyguards were shot down and he found himself more or less alone—I, as always, was hanging back, waiting to see what developed. Egged on by Hector, the Trojan rank and file hurled themselves at Achilles, who disappeared in the mass of them. I was going to cry out that they should come and fight me instead—I had a clear path back to the encampment— but their ranks shattered as Achilles burst out of them, spear whirling, his harsh metallic war-cry ringing, and for a moment I thought that this could not be a man, that this could only be the god of war. He slew many, sent the rest flying, and, best and last, drove his spear through great Hector's jaw.

I expected him to pursue the survivors but he just stood there, leaning on his spear. I found him grey-faced and trembling, his left foot soaked in gore—he had finally been wounded and it was a bad one, the tendon in his left ankle slashed through. I put his arm over my shoulder and helped him hobble back to camp. The physicians dressed the wound but it got infected and when I went to visit him I could smell the gangrene. I pled with him to have the leg off as the physicians said he must, or perish, but he refused, saying death was better than life as a cripple, and so he remained intact, and on the third day he died.

This was five years into the war. Any sane man would

have called it a loss, or perhaps found some way to construe it as a victory, and gone home, but Agamemnon was immovable. I was not the only one who tried to talk him into decamping but we might as well have debated with a stone.

I decided to end the war on my own. Knowing we would never take the city, I decided to go straight for the war's cause, so one night I put on beggar's rags and snuck into Troy with a bag of gold and a skinning knife. I went to the palace and lingered on the steps, begging alms of passersby (many of whom I recognized from the field, none of whom gave me a second glance). Helen passed by with her maids, all slaves, three Achaeans among them.

That night I slept under an abandoned market stall, stray dogs and adulterers padding by me. The Greeks probably thought I had deserted but I was both braver and more treacherous than they supposed. Early the next morning one of the Achaean maids came out to do her marketing. I fell into step behind her and, when opportunity arose, dragged her into an alley with my hand over her mouth. "Don't scream, sister," I said in Greek. "I have gifts, first gold and then your freedom, and in exchange I only want a little gold of another kind." I told her what to do to earn her passage home. She said nothing but took the bag and the knife and I saw in her eyes that she was a viper, that she hated Helen and her bondage and would do the dreadful thing I asked.

I crept back to the Greek camp and was asked no questions. The next night the maid was dragged to my tent by a guard who had found her wandering within our perimeter. She gave me a dark canvas sack within which was a mass of tangled, blood-spattered blonde hair with chunks of scalp still attached. The tone and richness of the hair identified it as the locks of none other than Helen of Troy, late of Sparta, no longer the most beautiful of women in respect of her recent death and mutilation but for all I knew the loveliest of ghosts. I noticed the brown crust under the maid's fingernails and called for a bath, telling her the hot water would wash away her bondage as the sea would wash away all indignities over the course of her imminent trip home.

That evening I called a general assembly. With the heat of the bonfire on my back and the eyes of every Greek on me I told them that in one of my fits Athena had revealed that though Troy could not be taken, the war could be won. My announcement was greeted with hoots of derision. Loud voices wondered how this was possible. I shouted, "By bringing an end to the cause of this war, to Helen of the house of Tyndareus!" And I held up her hair, instantly recognizable in the firelight. A moan went up from the men and Menelaus leapt to his feet trembling, knocked over his wine-cup and called for a sword, a sword. I threw her hair at his feet, saying, "Your wanton wife is dead and there's your honor cleansed. The war is won, let us go home." The Spartans gathered around him and some fool put a blade in his hand. The rest of the men gathered behind me, homesick and warsick, and turned hard gazes on the Spartans.

I had hoped that the Spartans, outnumbered, would back down. Menelaus and Agamemnon would bear me a grudge till the end of their days but let them, in everyone else's eyes I would be a hero—Odysseus, who had won the war at a stroke and abased the High King's pride. Unfortunately I had underestimated Spartan discipline and the hold the Spartan kings had on their men. They got their arms and my followers got their arms and battle was imminent when the Trojans attacked.

There must have been a spy in our camp—they could hardly have found a more vulnerable moment. We were disorganized, distracted, half-armed, at odds with each other and tightly clustered. They rushed us from all sides. The fighting was bitter and in the first minutes I thought we would be overwhelmed. I fought my way away from the bonfire and found a store-tent to hide in as shrieking filled the night behind me.

The night passed with glacial slowness except when I cut the throat of a Trojan soldier who came in looking for spoil. I had hoped that our numbers would outweigh their initiative but by the time the false dawn lit the sky things were not much quieter—the Trojans were making an all-out effort to break us. It is strange to say that it occurred to me to find my men and rally them to the banner of the Laertides but I quickly suppressed this pointless impulse.

I borrowed the dead Trojan's bloodstained cloak and helmet, reluctantly left the relative security of the tent and made for the camp's edge. Trojans saw my helmet and assumed I was one of them. Greeks made to attack me till I hailed them in their own language. I passed a few knots of melee, my brothers in arms doing noble deeds and dying. I was terrified for my own life and did nothing to help them, though the circumstances of their deaths are etched in my memory. I clambered over the rude timber walls at the camp's boundary and dropped down onto the sand below. From within the wall came cries of agony and the roar of flames—the Trojans must have gotten at the ships. Without, all was peaceful—a wide empty beach stretched before me and Troy was just visible on my left. It seemed unnatural that I could leave so easily. I threw my borrowed helmet into the surf and started walking.

After an hour the war seemed as though it had been a dream. I looked back and saw black pillars of smoke over the camp and over Troy.

I took stock of my situation. I had a sword, bread and a bag of silver. I was on a coast where I had no friends and many enemies, though few of them knew my name. Having no alternative, I kept walking south along the shore. I had heard of a city not far from Troy and in two days reached it. The guard at the gate asked me who I was and what I wanted. I had a mad impulse to say, "I am a sinister-minded foreigner who has lately been making war on the principal city of your country in hopes of rapine, pillage and blood-soaked revenge," but instead said I was an itinerant bard hoping to sing for my supper. The guard looked at my sword and said I carried a strange sort of lyre. I replied that bandits abounded, many of them desperate and dangerous renegades from the war up north, and I had discovered by trial and error that it was more effective to hit them with a sword than a musical instrument. Indeed, my lyre had not survived the first trial but I was pleased to say my sword was in good shape even after many encores—my most popular ballad was "Feint Toward the Heart and Slash the Hamstring" but "Throw Sand in Their Eyes and Stab the Sword-Hand" was gaining popularity.

I found a place with the lord of the city. I had been afraid it would be galling to sit at the lower table but in the event found a bard's station unobjectionable—I was given all I needed and there was no offensive familiarity. At first I sang the old standbys—"Theseus in the Repeating Labyrinth," "The Tale of Medusa's Shade," "Athena's Lover" and the like. I had the rapt attention of everyone from the lord to the potboy. Even the dogs under the tables watched with heads cocked.

Refugees trickled in over the following weeks and from their accounts I pieced together the story of the war's end. The Trojans had overplayed their hand—they set fire to the Greek ships but in their race to the shore left many Greek soldiers behind them, intact and desperate. Diomedes, an independent-minded Greek general, wrote off the ships as a loss and had his soldiers mount up and race for Troy, emptied of men, its gates hanging open. The Greeks erupted into the city and gave vent to their rage. When the Trojans saw the smoke they rushed home to stop the sack and hours and then days of vicious house-to-house fighting followed, until Troy and the Greek ships were all in ashes, the soldiers slain or scattered, both forces broken. The only Greek ship to survive was Agamemnon's, which had been anchored out in the bay—he and a handful of men sailed away that night, their sails filled with the spark-laden wind pouring out of the burning city, leaving their countrymen to get home as best they could.

I was concerned that the refugees would recognize me but no one thought to look for a Greek captain in the face of the bard sleeping on sheep-skins by the hearth. Still, when a month had passed the city was thick with displaced Trojans and I decided to go.

There were few bards that far out on the periphery of the Greek-speaking world and I flourished. I never failed to get applause when I gave them the classics and soon became confident enough to invent material. I never went as far as sussing out the local headman's lineage and singing a paean—I preferred to keep an emotional distance from my patrons. I took to telling the story of Odysseus of the Greeks, cleverest of men, whose ruses had been the death of so many. (In the same moment I formulated this epithet, it occurred to me that it was Helen's treacherous maid who told the Trojans when to attack. I wondered whether she was wealthy now or dead, or perhaps both, lying in a beehive tomb with gold and wine jars piled around her.)

It was when I was a guest in Tyre that I first heard another bard singing one of my songs and it occurred to me that I had in my hands the means of making myself an epic hero. What good is the truth when those who were there are dead or scattered? I took to rearranging the events of Troy's downfall, eliding my betrayals and the woman-killing, and making a good tale of it. My account of Odysseus's heroics changed according to my mood. Sometimes I led the defence as the Trojans went to burn the ships, sometimes I put myself in Diomedes' boots and led the counter-attack on Troy. Sometimes Athena loved me so much that she shattered the Trojan curtain wall with a thunderbolt.

Diomedes' cavalry, the maid's bag of gold and the hours hiding in the airless tent combined somehow to give me the idea of Greek soldiers ensconced in a treacherous wooden house. The ruse appealed to me and though I could never come up with a fully satisfactory reason why the Trojans would blithely drag a suspicious fifty-foot-tall wooden statue into their city, I glossed over their deliberations and the story was well received. I told the story so many times that I sometimes thought I really remembered Menelaus breathing fast and shallow in the stuffy darkness of the horse's belly.

I traveled widely and won much acclaim. I lived among other men but was not of them and this suited me precisely. On the island Chios I bought a gentleman's farm where I passed the winters. There were women, sometimes the same one for years, but I never married any of them and their names ran together.

In the tenth year after leaving Ithaca I realized I was done with singing and with new shores and cities. I gave the Chian farm to my woman at the time, and there were no hard feelings when I left for port and hitched a ride on a Phoenician trader bound in the general direction of home. At sea I lay on my back on deck and stared at the grey skies while composing an account of the last five years. From a muscle-bound Scythian brigand who had caught me stealing cheeses from his cave I made a one-eyed cannibal ogre. From the cold winters on Chios when I spoke with no one but my lover I made island imprisonments with kindly witches (there are, as far as I have seen, and I have seen much, no gods, no spirits and no such thing as witches, but I seem to be the only one who knows it—the best I can say for the powers of the night is that they make good stories).

At last the traders dropped me on the Ithacan shore and I hid my chests of gold in a cave I remembered. I cast my old cloak into the woods and using a tide-pool for a mirror shaved off the beard I had started when I landed on Asian shores. Clean-shaven, I looked absurdly young. I strode off to my father's hall and the predictable kerfuffle ensued—amazement, tears, glad reunions, questions, more tears, feasts, speeches. Tedium. I played my part as best I could but in truth just wanted it to end so I could spend my remaining years with sword and harp on the wall, making loans at high interest and fathering sons. I never sang again, fearful of being recognized, but I got some second-hand fame as a patron of bards. I was most generous when they had my songs word-perfect.

19

KILLING SCYLLA

The witch Circe told me that there was no fighting Scylla but it was not in me to believe her. Circe saw the set of my jaw and repeated herself—"She will take six of your men from the deck and it is not, cannot be, in your power to stop her. Don't waste lives dallying and trying to fight—just row by as quickly as you can. She is born of pure force and is not for you to contend with." I bowed and spoke graceful words that I could not afterward recall, as I was wondering how to kill Scylla.

A week out of Aiaia* we were in a narrow channel between high, guano-streaked cliffs where, Circe had said, Scylla lived. As the ship coasted along I armed myself in silence, ignoring Circe's counsel and the men's questioning looks. I wanted to tell my crew that I was poised to make a famous killing but held my tongue, scanning the cliffs for the lair I knew was hidden among the vortices of seabirds.

---

*Circe's island.

I almost missed it when she struck. I was looking out at the restless twitching waters on the other side of the channel and by luck glanced over my shoulder in time to see six men snatched up, Scylla's long necks twining and receding high above, gone in moments. The crew only realized what had happened when they heard the victims' cries, shrill and desperate, soon silenced. I gave the order to row at double time and they willingly obeyed. The spear in my hand was an absurd comfort as we passed out of range.

We made landfall on Apollo's island* and I sat in a black study with my face in my hands while the men crept silently about their duty. I suppressed the urge to sail straight back with bared teeth and drawn blade and instead meditated on her weaknesses, foremost among them her immobility. Pure defense is untenable—it cedes the initiative and even the strongest fortress could, as I had shown, be broken.

Circe had told me that the sun god prized his cattle, so I waited until nightfall before having them slaughtered. For all I knew, Apollo slept like everyone else. If he objects, I thought, let him come to Ithaca and I will give him back an equal number of cows and half as many again, for the Laertides are nothing if not generous. In any event, what's one more enemy on Olympus? In high

---

*On Apollo's island were his sacred cattle, which were immortal, or at any rate ageless, and which he prized highly.

good humor, I told the men that the cattle of the Sun would be a proper funeral sacrifice for the fallen and the means of our revenge into the bargain. They were reluctant to do the butchering, their mouths full of hesitant piety, so I grabbed a knife and cut the first cow's throat myself. As the blade slid in I thought, "This is not who I am, and this is not the way to a happy old age on Ithaca," but already the victim's steaming blood spattered my hands and its knees buckled and I was committed. The next cow was dragged forward and I told the men to heat up our forge.

All night we hammered spear blades into barbed hooks, then welded them to long chains affixed to my ship's keel. We arrayed the cattle's carcasses on deck in poses of sleep, the hooks concealed within their bodies, the chains covered with sailcloth. In the morning the fleet sailed within sight of Scylla's rock. We gave the deck of the slaughter-ship a last sluicing and pointed it toward the monster's lair. The men raised the sails and climbed down into a waiting boat—I locked the rudder and followed them down as the sails filled and the ship went off unmanned.

"The power of a god and the intelligence of a wasp," I thought as we rocked on the waves. "If this fails I will come back next year with something better. And if I die, then killing this animal will become the pastime of my son and his sons and every lord of Ithaca and my shade will not rest till they burn her heart before my tomb." We were half a mile away when her heads shot out from her cave to engulf the bait and still I flinched.

She tried to draw up her catch but the hooks bit, the chains held and she was abruptly brought up short. The ship rose slightly in the water but the breeze held and pulled her necks taut as lyre strings. I shivered at her wet, almost musical shrieking as her corpulent body was slowly pulled out of her cavern and into the sunlight, her claws scrabbling for purchase on the guano-slimed stone of her aerie till she reached the edge, clung for a moment, overbalanced and plummeted toward the churning sea where she landed with the sound of a siege-stone hitting a wall and disappeared under a mountain of foam.

I brought the boat forward, my spear poised for the coup de grâce, ready to gloat over her death agony. Her huge yellow body floated belly-up on oily waves, her heads bobbing around her, her fanged mouths slack and black eyes sightless.

I raised my spear but hesitated because among the tangle of her necks I saw a seventh head, not a monster's but a young woman's, with milk-white skin and sodden filthy hair. She caught my eye and shouting to be heard over the wind said, "You are the fate that has been haunting me since I was born. I huddled in my high cave for fear of you, starving and wretched, venturing out only to snatch a little food when I could. I thought of hiding in a deep cavern or on a high mountain but I was too afraid to leave home. Mine has been a miserable life and now it is ending and I wish I had never heard the name Odysseus."

DEATH AND THE KING

Graceful young men and women moved in small groups over the gentle slopes of Mount Ida, circulating around the temple of Quickness* where Helen sat receiving suitors with gracious brevity and a marble smile. The three most eminent bachelors were Odysseus, unmatched for intelligence, Agamemnon, who would one day be king of all Mycenae, and his brother Menelaus, who never quit.

Her father Tyndareus had been in a quandary, as he had just the one daughter but could not afford to offend the many princes who must necessarily go home bache-

---

*In the eighteenth century B.C. there was a thriving cult of the goddess Quickness, known for virginity, quick thinking, harsh laughter and an association with owls. Her particular enemy was Death, with whom she had fought a number of inconclusive wars, her object in which seems to have been eradicating his kingdom and ushering in an era of immortality. Her cult was immensely popular but such was the ruggedness of montane Greece that it soon speciated into a dozen subgenera. By the twelfth century B.C. her incarnation as Pallas Athena had displaced all others and is now remembered to the exclusion of her sisters. Quickness was a more lively goddess than Athena, open to human sacrifice and, in contrast with her sister, as much a user and a predator as a lover of heroes.

lors. He had therefore abdicated the decision to the goddess, and, to forestall future problems, had made each suitor swear that, should Helen be kidnapped, he would go to war to help recover her. As the suitors assembled on the temple steps, a white heifer was led out of the coolness of the shrine and stood blinking in the sun. Tyndareus said, "The groom will be the one closest to the victim," and cut the beast's throat. Odysseus, who was devoted to Quickness and confident of his chances, peered into the shadowy precincts of the temple and saw the idol smile at him with pity and affection and then turn her gaze toward Menelaus. The cow hesitated, then took a few tottering steps toward Menelaus and collapsed at his feet, wetting his thighs with her blood, and the suitors felt that there was a stranger among them. Helen laughed delightedly, either at the death or their dismay, and in the clarity of disappointment Odysseus realized that this was the first time he had seen her show emotion. It also occurred to him that however close Menelaus had been to the dying animal, Death was closer.

Menelaus took Helen back with him to Sparta but there was no peace in his victory because as soon as he was home the dreams began. Every night he dreamed he flew in lazy circles high over a dark place where he knew there was but could not see a city. Scattered points of light appeared, moving inward. He flew lower and the lights became torches in the hands of soldiers and then the city started burning, the army swarming in over the walls like sparks flowing back into a fire. He lost sight of the soldiers in the thickening smoke and tried to go lower. Then the wind changed and he was on the ground again and the soldiers lay dead around him, their bodies already stiff and pale though they showed no outward wounds. He walked among the bodies for a while and then he was on the walls of the now silent polis. Looking down (he knew he should not but could not help himself), he saw that the walls descended into the earth endlessly, vertiginously, layer upon layer of cold stone stretching down into darkness forever.

Every night he woke from this dream weeping but dried his tears before Helen could see them. Ashamed, he swore never to be afraid of mortal men or of the gods or even of death. As his wedding day receded into the past the dream faded but his resolve did not. He acquired the habit of smothering his fear with reckless bravado— he dove deeper than his friends in the coastal seas, rode breakneck over rough hills and more than once went first over an enemy wall, made so fast by terror that no spear or sword could touch him. By the time he was twenty* he believed he had conquered fear and valued himself highly for it. It was pride in his courage that made him open his gates to King Death, who, though famous for his hospitality, was used to getting none in return.

---

*At the time, Achaean men would marry around fifteen and Achaean women around twelve, so this would be well into his married life.

Death, who in those parts most often went by the name Paris, was a tall pale man with colorless eyes and flaxen hair. At first glance he looked like a thirty-year-old who had never been in the sun but the translucence of his skin, the formality of his bearing and the perfect blankness of his eyes made him upon consideration seem older, and older, and finally as old as night. He showed up at the palace gates without any retainers, clad in old black armor, knocking rhythmically and loud. The porter demanded his name and country and got a quiet answer. He went trembling to Menelaus and told him who had come. Menelaus did not hesitate, though he became very grim, and went out through the now empty courtyard to admit his guest.

Death must have been unaccustomed to a guest's portion but he played his part with courtesy. When the wine came, he poured a libation to Zeus the All-Father, who some said was his brother, saluted Menelaus and his knights and bowed to Helen, whose radiance seemed to light up the dark and smoky hall, though it and she were tolerably cold. As courtesy required, Menelaus spoke first of his own affairs, but when the wine was down to the dregs he asked the pale man how things did in his kingdom. Death said that though he was the ruler of but a single city he had many subjects and none had yet complained for want of room. He spoke of vast, heavy silence, of shadows moving over fields of asphodel, of the somnolent trickling of the waters of Hell, of the company of the august dead—Minos the judge, wise in all things, bluff Orion hunting the spirits of animals through the endless gloaming, and the mortal part of Hercules standing in the River Styx and looking pensively toward Mount Olympus, where his immortal twin disported himself among the gods. Finally Death said that for all he was master of shadows he had of late begun to pine for brightness, and with a sidelong glance at Helen rose and went away to his room.

That night Menelaus lay uneasily next to Helen. He dreamed that Death came into their chamber like winter. Death's eyes were cold and bright, his breath was frost, his armor was the void and now there was no mistaking him for a man. Death leaned over Helen and whispered in her ear. Menelaus could not quite make out what he said but his mind was full of dead suns, ancient cities made of ice, cold still things, quiet and thoughtful, on the edge of slipping into nothing. Of falling forever. Death drew her up out of bed and pulled her face into his chest and the dream faded.

In the morning Helen was gone and so was his guest—not only that but the wine he had drunk was spilled on the flags of the banquet hall and his meat lay on the bench unchewed, the dogs shunning it. Menelaus strapped on his sword and rode to see Agamemnon, now the High King, to tell him he meant to bring war to Death's city.

Menelaus and Agamemnon invoked the betrothal

oath and called up all the men who owed them service. They told their recruits only that Helen was gone and that they were making war on a great king in the East to get her back. The most intractable and desirable recruit was Odysseus, who had in the years since the wedding kept to Ithaca, his island kingdom, and spent his days in contemplation in Quickness's shrine.

Menelaus went to Ithaca, found Odysseus at prayer and demanded that he arm himself and come with him. Without getting up, Odysseus observed that he was indifferent to Menelaus's domestic problems and that in light of Menelaus's bad breeding Helen had probably left of her own accord, thereby negating the compact. Menelaus, implacable, said that he would bind Odysseus and bring him as a slave if not as a companion. Odysseus invited him to try and blood was in the air when on impulse Menelaus told him the name of the personage with whom he quarreled. Odysseus hesitated, glanced at his altar, sighed and said, "Your enemy is a terrible one but it seems I must go with you," and took his spear down from the wall.

They left Ithaca on a mirror-clear night, the ships sweeping through black water and reflected stars. Soon the dark hulls ground on the sands of Ilium, Death's country, the white sails were furled, and they leapt down onto the shingle with weapons in hand. The sand crackled underfoot—Odysseus scooped up a handful and saw that it was made up of ground bone, tiny fragments of tooth, skull and vertebrae. They pitched their tents on the shore in the shadow of Ilium's tall jagged walls and the odor of the charnel smoke rising from its towers. The augurs stared forlornly at the birdless sky.

The next morning the Greeks mustered to attack. As they drew near Ilium's massive gate and spike-surmounted walls they wavered, even Agamemnon hesitating, but Menelaus was indifferent both to his men and to terror and he led the way, eyes shining, without looking back to see if they followed. Passing the black tree growing before the gate of Ilium, Menelaus struck the gate three times with the pommel of his bronze sword.

A fog came down on them just as they were bringing up their battering ram—on that much, everyone afterwards agreed. From there, the stories diverged. Some spoke of stumbling out of the fog onto an endless plain of frost where they wandered for days without seeing any evidence of living things except, sometimes, their own footprints. Some found a palace woven of giant bones from which rushed grey warriors with grim faces who shrugged off even the cruelest blows. Others spoke of a grey devil sitting on a stone who sang dirges in answer to their shouted questions.

Many Greeks died in battle but some of them came back to take their places in line with the living, their wounds still open but no longer bleeding. Menelaus did not like it but he did not fall short of men. Sometimes Death's army sallied forth from Ilium, full of rage, but their passion was quickly spent and often his soldiers would stop in the middle of battle as though transfixed by a sudden inspiration, their gazes fixed on the horizon, motionless, even as the rejoicing, vindictive Greeks hacked them to pieces.

The high walls of Death's city became the ubiquitous background of the Greeks' dreams. There was a universal sense of oppression to which only Menelaus was immune—he fought with delighted abandon, never giving ground, always attacking. He would face a thicket of spears alone if his men's courage failed, but he was never wounded or even tired. His tent was the only one in camp from which laughter was heard and his recklessness and apparent contempt for his enemy gave heart to his soldiers. Agamemnon strove to follow his brother's example, and though he could not be as careless he fought valiantly against the soldiers of Death—he cursed and roared, hacked through cold flesh, caught them and bound them and burned them in pits.

As for Odysseus, Quickness carried him. When he was a child he had seen her frequently—she had played games with him in the woods behind his father's house and instructed him in the use of the bow. She had been more reticent since he had grown up, only appearing to him when he killed his first man and once after five days of fasting. Now he could always feel her with him, hovering nearby him in battle, turning aside arrows and stones, whispering in his ear when to push the attack and when to flee. One night as he resharpened his sword, dull from hacking through the stiffened sinews of the dead, he asked her why, since she protected him, she did not commit herself fully and blast his enemies with lightning? She said nothing but he could feel her amusement and had the sense that she was biding her time.

The war dragged on. Clouds hid the sun for months at a time and the warriors' tanned faces turned pale. Not all the apparitions were enemies—Agamemnon swore that when he had been cornered by Ilium's gates his long-dead great-grandfather had appeared, hefted his old boar-spear and laughed while he spitted the menacing ghouls. Menelaus lost weight and there were black rings under his eyes but he never faltered in his singularity of purpose. As for Odysseus, he woke one morning to a strange sound—he went into the tent next to his and found Karéte, a second cousin on his mother's side, alabaster pale and drawing each bubbling breath through a long gash in his throat (which had been made by a left-hander, some part of Odysseus's mind noted, and a strong one). The cut was not bleeding and Karéte turned restlessly in his sleep. Odysseus went back to his tent, lit a stick of incense before Quickness's idol and begged her to show him how to end the war.

She answered instantly, as though she had been waiting for him to ask. He heard her out and for the first time presumed to argue with her, but she would not be moved.

He duly went to the black tree before Ilium's gates. Standing on a stone, he tied a rope to its lowest branches, knotted it around his neck, closed his eyes, and, commending his soul to Quickness, jumped. Though he had surreptitiously frayed the rope in hopes of it breaking, it held, and darkness overtook him. When he came to, it was night and he lay on the ground beneath the tree wearing a torque of rope. Ilium's gates hung open and he stole silently in.

Within the walls of the dead city all was still though the night was full of tension. Now and then high falsetto singing drifted up through sewer grates and he quickened his pace, soon coming to the center of the city where Death's dour palace loomed. It had high windows but no doors and its seamed facade reminded Odysseus of a mouth sewn shut.

He climbed up one of the cracks in its face to a small window just wide enough to squeeze through. He could see nothing of the dark room within but heard a faint whispering. He dangled by his hands and let himself fall into blackness, landing heavily and scrambling up, groping blindly, finding nothing. The room felt empty, like an abandoned warehouse, but as his eyes adjusted he made out a tall black throne beside which Helen sat on a footstool. Odysseus tugged at the rope around his neck and knelt before her in the gloom (noticing with a twinge that her beauty had not dimmed), begging her to leave with him and end the awful war but she barely seemed to see him, continuing a low monologue (this was the whispering he had heard) about the vast night of Paris's eyes and how he, ever the gentleman, had not yet touched her, though she had wanted him to. Odysseus cajoled and reasoned. He pled for his life and the lives of all the Greeks, her kinsmen among them. He revealed the command he had been given by Quickness, who was implacable. But she did not attend and Odysseus, exasperated, full of horror and rage, drew his sword, pulled her head back by the hair and cut her throat. He threw down the sword, the clang as it hit the ground obscene in such a quiet place, and staggered away.

Paris stepped forward (he had always been there, Odysseus realized, but unseen) and gently picked up her body. As he held her she spasmed and drew a long shuddering breath. In that moment Quickness appeared with a feral hateful grin and fell upon Death with a howl. She crushed him close and wrapped her strong white fingers around his throat and in the moment before they disappeared Odysseus saw dismay on Death's face. Though Quickness was gone, her war-cry echoed in the dismal hall. Odysseus fled then, getting a last glimpse of Helen crawling slowly away, leaving a trail of bloody handprints behind her.

There was a door to the outside that he hadn't seen

before. He ran through it and straight to the unguarded city gates. He threw them open and called out to Menelaus to come and get his revenge if he wanted it. Menelaus and Agamemnon came running, eyes blazing, their army close behind, and rushed into the city. The listless dead pulled themselves out of the vaults and sewers to resist them but with Paris gone the defence was apathetic and the Greeks carved through them with élan.

In the uncountable mausoleums were many funerary offerings, among them jars of strong wine, and even before victory was certain the soldiers were drunk, mouths stained red, draping themselves in rotten thousand-year-old finery and pausing in their bloody work to chase after the marmoreally cold empty-eyed girls who watched from alleyways. For all that, the Greeks soon broke their enemies and built a great fire in Ilium's square to burn them.

Before the bonfire Menelaus declared to his cheering men that Paris was dethroned, that Ilium would be razed and a new city built over its ruins. He would anoint himself the new king, break Death's dominion and open the kingdom of shadows to the sun. He went to Death's palace to get Helen but found only sticky red hand-prints and an overturned stool.

When all Paris's soldiers had been turned to ash, Menelaus did as he had sworn and took Death's throne. His commands rang through the onyx halls of Ilium and though the soldiers could have gone home then, every man chose to stay, except Agamemnon, who made a short trip back to Greece to see his wife.*

Menelaus passed his days in the citadel, reading Death's book and walking his halls. When the moon shone just so on his great black throne there sometimes came a clattering from below and a white, pure light would shine up through a grating in the floor. In a bubbling voice with just the barest trace of her old music Helen would then speak to him, telling him the gossip of the underworld that was now her home, of the basements and dungeons stretching down below the city, the extremities of whose depths were even for her just a rumor. So Menelaus had his wife, though he never set eyes on her, and his revenge, though not by his own hand, and his enemy's throne, though it was a terrible one. In due course he set out to add to his kingdom.

As for Odysseus, he slipped out of the city during the sack and took ship for Ithaca alone. He had hoped for a quick passage home but found himself opposed by strong winds and thick fogs. He found many islands but all were abandoned.

He was walking through still cold water toward a grey beach when Quickness appeared to him for the last time. She floated in the air, naked now and taller (he had never seen her naked before—she was as well made as he had

---

*Upon returning from the Trojan War, Agamemnon was murdered by his wife, Clytemnestra.

imagined but seemed to have somehow moved beyond beauty or its absence), and sparks glowed in her hair. She touched his face (somehow he could not imagine her talking now). She looked viciously happy. Her eyes met his and then she disappeared and he was left wondering.

21

HELEN'S IMAGE

Years before the Trojan War, King Tyndareus decided it was time to marry off his daughter Helen and, as she was the same age, her cousin Penelope. Penelope was fair but Helen, who was actually the daughter of Zeus, though no mortal but her mother knew it, had beauty that broke men's wills. Upon hearing of Helen's impending introduction to society, the flower of Achaea's bachelorhood descended on Tyndareus's palace to court his favor and (since he was an indulgent father) his daughter's. Odysseus, young and ambitious, came all the stormy way from Ithaca to win her, but when he arrived and saw the throng of suitors surrounding the girls he knew that for all his skill in war and presence of mind, his kingdom was small and poor, and more eligible princes abounded. Pensive, he haunted the periphery of the hall where Helen suffered gentlemen to wait on her and racked his mind for a stratagem. He was distracted by the braying laughter of Menelaus, a thick-headed bully whose ill breeding was evident in the offhand contempt with which he treated Penelope, who hovered near him, her eyes fixed on his face, filling his wine cup and laughing at jokes intended for Helen.

"I must have Helen or die," Odysseus thought, "though she does not seem like the sort of thing that can be had. More like a raptor, bright-eyed, poised over the world, inaccessible, rarely descending, swiftly striking. It would be worth my life to get her." Just then Mentor, Odysseus's father's man who had come with him from Ithaca, appeared as though from out of a mist and pulled him aside. Eyes shining, Mentor said he had noticed that though every man was smitten with Helen and could scarcely tear his eyes from her face, no two of them described her the same way. This effect was so pronounced that they might have been describing different women altogether. For Agamemnon she was wide-hipped, cow-eyed, faithful and slow. For Themistocles she was a wild thing of volatile moods and for Idomenos a giddy, vapid admirer of his seamanship, and so on.* Not only that but when she was not immediately before them her suitors were hard-pressed to remember anything about her at all—he had found that when Helen was out

---

*Helen, though mortal, was more god than not. The ichor of her father Zeus had bred truer in her than in any of his other mortal scions; in consequence of her fractional godhead, no mortal man could look upon her without being burned away, until Zeus took pity on her (and perhaps on the Achaeans) and hid her behind a veil that occluded most of her nature—any man looking at her would see the epigone of feminine beauty as he conceived it, and almost nothing of who she really was (in so far as she was anyone at all).

of sight her suitors could not even recall the color of her hair, although they accepted any suggestion given to them. Menelaus the Spartan was the only one who was not smitten with her—he seemed to desire her because she was considered desirable and only the best wife was consistent with his dignity. Odysseus, skeptical, tried to remember her face and failed. A plan formed and in his preoccupation he did not notice when Mentor vanished in a rushing of wings.*

That night Odysseus climbed up the wall of the palace garden through thick perfumed air and into Penelope's bedroom. She regarded him morosely, dull-eyed and indifferent at the prospect of ravishment. Odysseus sat beside her on her bed, put an arm around her shoulders and asked in a conspirational whisper how would she would like to have Menelaus for a husband. Penelope replied with the clarity of depression that she would like it above all things but that no one could compete with Helen. Odysseus said, "I will get you what you want, and as for Helen she will get a husband who is a much better man than Menelaus."

The next morning Tyndareus's valet brought him a note that had been found in the banquet hall. It was from Helen, informing him that she had fallen in love with

---

*It is interesting to note that Odysseus's description of Helen consists mostly of attributes characteristic of Pallas Athena. Mentor was one of Athena's preferred manifestations—one wonders whether she was aware of what Odysseus saw and whether even her fortress-like heart was moved a little.

Menelaus, prince of Sparta, and had asked him to carry her away that night, this being the only sure way of getting the husband she wanted. In a postscript she conveyed her kindest regards to the other suitors. As the young men grumbled over this effrontery the rumor spread that Penelope, the plain one, had also eloped, going off with an obscure island-lord. Tyndareus sat fuming until he realized that both his wards were in advantageous marriages, that he had not paid a single copper in dowry and that no one could say a word against him.

On Ithaca, Odysseus's bride was his delight and for her part she did not seem to mind him, though she would never let him see her undressed. In Sparta, Menelaus was happy because he had what everyone else wanted. For the first few months of their marriage his wife adored him, but soon even she found him odious. He reciprocated her dislike and, still loath to let anyone else so much as see her, kept her sequestered in his palace.

When the glib and handsome Prince Paris visited the Spartan court, Penelope, who was permitted out of the women's quarters for state occasions, was easily seduced, absconding with him not so much for love as in hope of any other kind of life.

In due course Agamemnon and Menelaus came to Ithaca and demanded that Odysseus muster his forces to sail with them to recapture Helen. Odysseus longed to explain the joke and tell them to forget about their war and

go home somewhat the wiser, but he saw their grim faces
and their warships in the harbor and knew he would not
long survive that revelation, so he went home and kissed
Helen goodbye, waiting to see if she would kiss him in
return (he had lived with her for years by then but had
not yet made up his mind whether she liked him, nor
had he learned to read her face), and then got his arms to
go to the war that he hoped would end by summer's
reaping.

22

BRIGHT LAND

Pale* lived by the sea in an open house on high posts that the tide ran through. The house was full of light and while he had mother and sister, canoe, sun and sea he wanted for nothing but his father, who had been away at war in the East since time out of mind.

Every morning his sister dove for mussels in the shallows of the bay, his mother spun wool on her wheel, and he went fishing in his canoe. When the sun was straight overhead his mother put down her work and peered into the East in hopes of seeing her husband returning, but she only ever saw water and air. In the afternoon Pale and his sister walked in the forest or listened to their mother tell tales of the bright lands to the west where virtue flowed down from the tops of the mountains and evil washed in from the sea.

One day in an infinite succession of otherwise identi-

---

*There is a tradition, albeit present in only a few fragmentary sources, that Odysseus's son Telemachus was pale to the point of albinism.

cal days, the sky turned dark and the sea was angry and the air was like smoke. Pale was fishing in his canoe and as he was a brave man he kept casting his net, though he could not see out of the troughs of the waves. A great swell came out of the east and bore him up and up till he thought all the water in the sea must be flowing beneath him, and then it dropped him down. When he and his canoe bobbed to the surface, an evil intuition sent him racing toward shore over water that ran black and full of weed. The beach where his house had been was swept clean, nothing there but smooth, damp, white sand. The forest above the house was gone too, dying fish and sea-weed in its place, uprooted trees bobbing in the turbulent surf. He paddled frantically here and there looking for his mother and sister, thinking he saw hair floating on the surface and racing over only to find a tangle of kelp or a broken gull.

He was determined, but on the third day he gave up. He lay on his back and let the canoe drift, eyes closed, swimming in the blood-red light of the sun. At sunset he sighed and turned his back on the empty coast. He had heard that thirteen days' paddle to the south was an island where one-eyed wild men lived in caves, and he had heard that inland a track led through the forest and over the hills to a city with a high round wall where the king had never seen the sea, but he let night fall and set his course by the stars for the bright lands in the west, for if his mother and sister had gone anywhere it would be there, to bathe in the springs at the top of the mountains. The water glowed blue with each paddle stroke and he sang a wordless song through the turning of the night.

Toward dawn, he came to an islet with a spring and beached there to sleep through the day. He flipped over his canoe, crawled into its shade and was closing his eyes when he heard a hoarse crying. He sprang up and found a small seal floating in the tide, moving weakly. "Perhaps your family misses you, seal," he said and dragged it out of the water above the high tide mark into the shade of a surviving palm. He went to sleep and dreamed that he saw a slight woman with pitch black hair and bright black eyes smiling down at him. At dusk he woke and the seal was gone.

He filled his water jug in the spring, oriented by the dolphin constellation, and headed west. In the late watches of the night he thought he saw the seal again, keeping pace with him, but the seal, if there was a seal, soon dove and was seen no more.

By the tenth night he was out of water and bone-weary and there had been no land in a long time. Though it was hours till dawn he put up his paddle and rested, soothed by the swell and the wind. There was a splashing by the side of the canoe. He looked over and saw the young woman holding the side, smiling up at him, her mass of wet hair shining in the starlight. She said, "Where are you going, stranger so far from home?" "To the bright lands in the west," he replied, in what voice he had left, "where virtue flows from the tops of the mountains." "And evil flows in from the ocean," said she. "I know the place well, and you'll never get there in your little canoe. All you'll find is ocean and sky and never a sight of an island though you break your back with paddling. But I know the way and I can take you there, so take my hand and come along." He put down his paddle, which had grown very heavy, took her hand, and went over the side with her, disappearing into the warm sea with scarcely a ripple.

What happened then? In the end did his clean white bones float slowly down to settle on the abyssal plain, or did he marry her and become a prince of the seals, living in the deep and forgetting his life as a man, or did he one day drag himself through the surf onto what his heart knew at once for the bright lands? The sea does not tell.

23

ISLANDS ON THE WAY

Odysseus's ship rose in the water as his men carried the stolen treasure of many cities from its hold to his new hall. Alcinous, the island's king, stood by watching, well pleased with his son-in-law-to-be. As soon as Odysseus had unloaded the ship he hitched a team of oxen to it with strong cables and dragged it up onto the beach. He took a crackling pine torch and, heart sinking despite his resolve, held it to the beached ship's flank, but the sea-worn timber would not catch and the sun was setting so he went home. The next day was his wedding day, and then it took weeks to set his new house and lands in order, and by then the wind had covered the ship with sand and it was easily ignored.

Staying on the island had been a natural decision, reached in the course of all the frigid nights guiding the ship by the faint luminescence of the waves and the occasional glimpse of the moon through ragged cirrus. Somewhere in the Middle Sea the stars Odysseus had relied on for navigation had changed like ships come unmoored and after that he was altogether lost. Privately terrified, Odysseus had confidently told his men that this ominous event was just the gods translating new heroes into the sidereal sphere after the war in Troy. He pointed up and pretended to recognize Patroclus and Achilles (their constellations intertwined), Hector and even great, sad Ajax of Telamon. Then there were the seasons that did not seem to come when expected, though no one managed to keep an exact count of the days—hash marks on the hull rotted, a jar full of white stones was shattered in a storm, knotted leather threads turned into damp-swollen, hopelessly entangled snarls.

They saw many islands and many marvels, most of them inimical. One evening a sickly green radiance passed below them, deep among the waves, and the lookout swore it had had the shape of a man. On another night all their fires went out and every light, from the stars to the moon to the glow of the waves, disappeared in an instant. In total darkness they tried to turn the ship around, botched it, and before an hour had passed they were expecting to drift forever. Odysseus tossed a coin over the bow and there was no splash. They held themselves together in the dark by sitting on deck and telling stories, each in turn. They were never more surprised than when the sun rose.

Now and then they found an island set down on their

map. Invariably it had just been visited by Phoenician or Cretan merchants, elements of the world they knew, and Odysseus and his men took heart, got directions and advice, and sailed off in the expectation of finding familiar lands that never, in the event, materialized. And so, gradually, the longing for Ithaca's shores was supplanted by the wish for any kind of an end to wandering.

When Odysseus and his men washed up on Alcinous's island he received them graciously, being particularly attentive to Odysseus—he mentioned in passing that he had a daughter but had not yet found the right husband for her. Odysseus weighed the benefits of a new marriage against the open trackless sea and, his spirit much eroded, asked to meet her. A wedding was soon arranged and consummated and not long after the rest of the Greeks followed suit. They had children, bought land, acquired standing and thought less and less and finally never of their wives in Ithaca. They told and retold their travel tales so many times that they became less memories than fables, even to the tellers. The hardness of their youth and of the War left them slowly, but it left them, and eventually there was not a head among the crew that was not white and their swords gathered dust on their mantels.

Like their wandering, this seemed as if it must go on forever but ended abruptly. One night Odysseus had a dream that Athena was standing smiling over him, leaning on her spear, her eyes like white coals. He could feel the chill radiating from her. She had been speaking but he could not remember anything she had said, though his mind was full of a confusion of demons haunting narrow sea-lanes, a witch in silver bowers praying in a wolf's voice to the moon, and the echoing screams of men packed close in a low-ceilinged room as black arrows sprouted from their throats and hearts. She whispered, "It's time to go."

He sat up, wide awake—there was no one but his wife Nausicaa, asleep beside him. The moon shone full through the window and he was as alert as if it had been noon. Odysseus stood straight for the first time in years, throwing off the stoop that he now realized had been a concession to the expectations of age. He took his sword down from the wall, drew it and turned it in the moonlight, the metal flickering like water. He hesitated, enjoying the stillness of the house and regretting the warmth of Nausicaa's bed. Then he went out, closing the door carefully behind him and, leaning into the strong wind blowing through the empty streets, walked out of the city and along the strand to the spot where the ship had beached. The racing wind that threatened to tear his cloak away had exhumed it and a loose pennant flapped wildly on its mast. His surviving men were there, standing straight as pine trees, and he could not tell if the white in their hair was age or moonlight. Without a word, they set their shoulders to the ship and pushed it toward the sea, wallowing in the sand, redoubling their efforts as her hull touched water. They clambered aboard as the tide took her and pulled her past the breakers and out to sea, bound, they thought, for Ithaca.

ODYSSEUS IN HELL

A man picks his way along a steel cable strung over a refulgent blue abyss, a ship's oar over his shoulders for balance. The cable groans and sighs in the infinitesimal breeze. It is so narrow that the man is, when he thinks of it, surprised he is able to keep his footing. Miles in front of him the horizon is shrouded in bright clouds. It may well be the same behind him but he has never looked back. The cable sags, very slightly, just discernibly over the course of what may be hours, or days—he is descending.

Above him (he sees this out of his peripheral vision—to look up would be fatal) is an irregular dark massiveness suggesting mountains. There are iridescent patches that could be lakes or possibly cities. Below is open sky, gradations of deep featureless blue. Now a weariness comes over him and he stops to rest, squatting and balancing the oar across his shoulders, gripping the cable with feet and hands, peering down into the void in which he finds a measure of comfort.

He has been walking and balancing for a long time and his mind wanders. For the most part his reflections are vacant or circular recapitulations of the conditions of his confinement in this limitless open air. When a thought crystallizes it is this: Somewhere a judgment is being made. Even now advocates are striding in flapping robes through bleak arcades toward the ante-rooms where they will make their case before a judge, whose name he almost knows—Minos, or possibly Yama. This stirs something in his arid, empty mind—he wants to argue the case himself.

He knows that if the judgment goes against him a wind will rise in the west, a white rushing mass devouring a hemisphere of sky, racing over him and scouring the cable clean. He considers tactics for such a situation—leaning into the wind and walking on the windward side of the cable, or breaking into a dead run when he sees the storm rising, with every hasty step risking a sudden, final slip, though no end to the cable is in view. He recognizes the futility of these plans but this does not permit him to stop formulating them.

The cable might be getting narrower. His legs might be weakening. He might feel the air stirring. Eyes closed, he hesitates and imagines the languor of falling. He sees himself snatching futilely at the cable, missing, how quickly it would dwindle, and how he would at last have the luxury of looking up at the world he was falling away from, secure in the knowledge that whatever else came the worst had happened. He steadies himself and takes another step.

Once a generation the spring tide reaches the broken walls of Troy and it is granted him to recall that once he was Odysseus.

25

THE BOOK OF WINTER

I am not unhappy, despite the cold and the monotony. There are many things to love about this place—the susurrus of falling snow, the tracks of deer and hare encircling the house, the black rooks landing heavily on laden branches and sending down white showers. And at night the wolves prowl my doorstep, their fur crusted with snow, hungry winter revenants howling their hopeless laments. I dream of cold mists pouring from their open throats and enveloping the valley.

The days are full, and I am never bored. Most of my waking hours are spent in contemplation of my circumstances. My conclusions, so far, are these: someone built this cabin, stocked it with food and fuel, and furnished it, however sparsely. This much is obvious—not even the most active imagination would have it that this house, made of sawn planks, was a natural structure, or that the firewood had split itself, or that the many pounds of biscuit had grown in their sacks like a fungus. What I do not know is the identity of the builder. He has taken no pains to reveal himself, and quite possibly wishes to remain unknown.

He could have been a hunter who needed a forest lodge. He could have been a pioneer trying to cut a farm out of the woods, defeated in the end by the cold and the short days and the snow settling in drifts against the door. There are many possibilities that I have neither proved nor disproved, which stymies me, as the problem of the builder is logically prior to the other mysteries, such as the language of the wolves, what I will do when the biscuit runs out, and my own name.

My ignorance is upsetting but I calm myself by reasserting my faith in logic. There is no action under the sun that does not entail myriad effects, all of which leave signs, and from this chain of signs all previous actions can be inferred. Perhaps at some point one loses the trail of causation because of one's limited powers of thought or discernment, but building a house is a profoundly disruptive act—as with murder, there are a limited number of probable motivations.

The builder, however mysterious, has at least left a clear sign of his presence. What sign have I left? I have melted snow, eaten biscuits and burned firewood. But what else is there to do? I ask the rooks and they tilt their heads inquisitively, but say nothing.

I wonder if I am the builder. I do not know how to build houses, but I have forgotten a great deal—perhaps I have forgotten that as well. My hands are callused, but I cannot remember what it would feel like to lift a hammer. This does not mean I never knew. If I had tools I could use them and see if anything came back to me, or if they caused calluses and whether those calluses matched the ones I have now. Of course, I have no tools.

I have many scars, the largest one a long white slash on my thigh. I try to read them, hoping for a memory of some accident or battle, but they are illegible.

I wonder if I am a prisoner and this house is my jail. The door is always unlocked but I have only the one thin shirt—when I go outside the cold drives me back into the cabin within minutes. It would be a strange sort of prison that lasts only for a season, unless winter never ends here. I do not remember it beginning.

I have asked the wolves about these things. They listen with their tongues lolling, giving every appearance of thoughtful attention, but when I am done they trot off into the trees without comment. The hawks turn their bright eyes on me and seem concerned with my plight but they too are silent. I sometimes think the falling snow murmurs to me in a language I cannot quite understand.

The solution to my perplexity comes one morning when I ransack the cabin for what might be the hundredth time and on impulse drag the firewood bin away from the wall. Behind it I find a soot-smudged book coated with wood dust. I set it on the table and slowly rotate it, scrutinizing it from every angle, my breath quickening. Its binding is thick and pebbled and there is no title on the spine. Its pages are cut—someone has read it. I hope it is a diary, or a memoir, or at any rate some kind of an explanation. I open it reverently and read.

By dusk I have read the book through. It is the story of Odysseus, soldier and diplomat, a man of versatile intelligence who connived to destroy a sacred city in the East and made the long trip home over many trying years.

I wonder what the book was meant to tell me. The allegorical possibilities are many, and the number of codes it could conceal are infinite, but it could be a simpler, more nearly literal message—perhaps it is, in some small way, my story. I could be the orb-eyed cyclops in his cavern, for like him I am remote from mankind, and for all I know would be angry at visitors, but I have two eyes. I could be Telemachus, who is lost in his own land. I could even be Penelope, a prisoner in my home, courted by the cold wind and winter. Is my house Ithaca Hall? The Phaeacian castle? Are the wolves Scylla, the cold Charybdis?

I re-read the book. Once again it ends with Odysseus allaying Poseidon's wrath by walking inland with an oar over his shoulder until someone mistakes it for a winnowing fan. The shock of revelation is so great that I go out and stand for a minute in the cold, the sharp wind and harsh light making my eyes water, before coming back in to read the ending again. At last, I know myself. I hug myself with delight at having finally solved the riddle.

Modesty had kept me from believing it, or at least from admitting it to myself, but now all is clear. The essential insight is that the text is corrupt, or, if not corrupt, then incomplete, or of a calculated obscurity. Immortal Poseidon's wrath was implacable—in order for Odysseus to escape from his vengeance once and for all it was necessary that he cease to be Odysseus. What would the cleverest of the Greeks have done in that situation? He would have gone somewhere remote, far away from gods and men and, somehow, forgotten everything, and thereby been himself no more. I can only speculate on how he managed to attain his amnesia. I do not know that I would now have the courage to go through with it—I can see that already much has changed for me. And then, I would be most unwilling to let go of my revelation.

Perhaps he went through each scene of his life and held it fixed in his mind's eye until it disappeared. Eventually even his most vivid memories (the first time he touched Penelope's skin, falling overboard and gasping just as a wave broke over his face) would fade to burnt-out after-image. Then, perhaps, he contaminated and diluted the remaining fragments of memory, rearranging them in every possible permutation: Penelope as a vapid giggler with apple-green eyes, Penelope as a heavy immovable woman whose chief pleasure is resentment, Penelope as a young wanton who in middle age comes to cherish respectability above all things. Eventually, memory is subsumed in white noise.

Even this, though, would be not quite enough. There must have been some final discipline that destroyed the last vestiges of self, but, whatever it was, it was so thorough that I lack the capacity even to imagine it.

With relief, I open the stove and feed the book to the flames. It is the last link to who I was, and there is just enough left of me to see it. The book blackens, writhes and disappears. Now every debt is paid, every sin erased and I can begin anew, I who was once Odysseus and now am no one.

26

BLINDNESS

I could have lived among light and ambrosia, bright forever-young things coming and going on each other's arms and the wine and the night inexhaustible. But that world was flat to me, and for all that my father is great among them I wanted no part of it. Even if she had been true (I am not considered handsome, never have been) I think I would have preferred my island, my farm, and my solitude. I have never had the island altogether to myself but I made my neighbors dislike me from the first—from time to time a farm-wife dropped by as in duty bound but I offered no more than politeness required, or a little less, to ensure my privacy. Sometimes in the distance I heard a girl's sweet singing and I needed no more company.

I lived in a cave as it was easier than a proper house, cool in summer and warm in winter. I tended my goats, made cheeses, split firewood and fished. I fancied myself a philosopher although for the most part my philosophizing consisted of staring out to sea, usually with a fishing pole in my hand, thinking of nothing. The sun would

bore into my brain over the hours and drive out everything except a ringing brightness, making everything
look hollow or flat.

One day I came home and found my cave full of visitors. They had been regaling themselves on my larder and
greeted me with swollen-cheeked, stupidly beaming
faces, their lips greasy with my mutton, invoking the for-
mulas of guest friendship and waiting for their welcome.
I gave them no welcome but curses and, still sun-struck
and sea-addled, hit one of them with my staff. I only
meant to scare him but I have always been strong and he
fell and knocked his head on the wall with the sound of a
stone landing at the bottom of a deep well. They would
have taken him and gone (or tried to—my blood was up)
but their captain, who had a face full of guile, begged my
pardon, apologized for the intrusion, called me lord and
with all humility proffered a skin full of strong wine as a
belated host gift. It had been a long time since I had
tasted wine and I was a little mollified (not to mention
ashamed of myself for overreacting). We sat down to
drink, and for the sake of politeness I asked them who
they were and where they came from. The captain said
his name was Nobody (a strange moniker, I thought at
the time, but it would have been unseemly to comment)
and that he and his men had sailed from Crete to trade
for amber and linen but on their way had found nothing
but trouble—pirates of opportunity, perilous storms,
comrades washed overboard in the night and their course

lost these many months past. Nobody droned on about his adventures and sleep came to me as I sat watching him across the fire. How painful it is that his sly fox face was the last thing I ever saw.

I woke to blood and agony and darkness. Staggering to my feet, I lashed out and felt my fist connect with resilient flesh. I put my hands around the spear with which I had been mutilated; vitreous humor trickled down my face and I knew with nauseous certainty that I would never see again. I drew out the spear and lay about with it, feeling their bones crack through the shaft. I bellowed and pressed the attack, not caring if I blundered into an outstretched sword. Commotion, hoarse panicked voices and motion in every direction. With mortal intent I made a mighty thrust toward the closest whisper but struck the wall—the spear broke in two and I was left holding a fragment of the haft, just big enough for a torch. I stopped and listened—it was silent but for my heart and my breathing. They had gone.

I put my hands to my ruined face, then bound the wound as best I could and staggered down the steep path to the sea. I thought I heard their oars on the water and raged at them, wading out into the surf, flailing at the waves, finding stones by touch and hurling them. I might have heard Nobody's voice but with the breakers and my shouting I could not be sure.

They were gone and I got cold. I was not quite brave

enough to drown myself. I shouted for my father—I did not love him much but he knew his duty and I thought he would avenge me. If he heard me, he gave no sign. I crept back to my cave and the pain, which had been waiting at a distance, engulfed me.

Fever came. I lay by the fire, chilled to the bone, too weak even to go to the well. At first the fever was low and I was transcendently calm and thought I had at last found true philosophy. As the fever rose and rose I started to shake uncontrollably. A young man with golden hair appeared, standing patiently in the shadows, watching me, leaning on a staff around which snakes twined (of course, if there had been such a man, I would not have seen him). In the dream, as the pain deepened he came more and more into the light and I thought he would speak to me but just then my father arrived and sent him away. He laid his vast hand on my forehead, as cool as the deeps of the sea, and I told him that it was Nobody who did this to me and must die.

The fever broke soon after that and I lay awake and alone in my cave, facing a future of darkness. I groped in the dust and found cheeses, my staff, a bucket, the empty wineskin, the cold ashes of the fire, a pile of furs, and the sharp end of the spear that had blinded me, still sticky with dried blood and matter. I sat down and I think I would not have got up again if not for my goats, who butted their heads against me and clamored to be milked.

This I managed to do, and then shooed them off to their pasture and laid out their salt while they bleated and had their little quarrels.

The days were long and there was no sun to dazzle me. I wondered incessantly about the man who had brought me a sack of wine, a tale and blindness. In my mind I replayed everything he had said, trying to reconstruct each tone and nuance. He had not uttered a single true word, of course, but we are revealed in our lies. His and his men's clothes had been thrice-patched stuff but their helmets and arms were keen edged and mirror polished. They had carried their arms with a total casualness, their weapons extensions of themselves, like veterans old in war. They had accents, the like of which I had never heard before, so I reckoned Nobody and his men must be from far away, out toward the edge of the world.

My hatred of Nobody was impotent and all-encompassing. I wanted to be free of it, but always my mind went back to him. I told myself and the goats stories about him—one day he and his men were pirates from Corsica, vicious raiders out to prey on anyone they could overwhelm or surprise. The next they were a party of pilgrims bound for Delphi who had stopped on my island for water and found me only through misfortune. But their ragged clothes and gleaming weapons, their hardness and loneliness and hunger made me decide in the end that they were coming back from a long, bloody war, fought far from home, a war that left them with eyes as blank and hostile as birds of prey, raiding and killing as the opportunity arose, knowing no life but arms and no law but violence.

I invented perils for his trip home—horrors rising up from the deep sea, the endless asphodel fields of the dead, sweetly singing witches to gull and bind him—but I could never quite bring myself to finally close the sea over his head or the jaws on his throat. Always I pulled him back, unwilling to let him escape into death. As his trials mounted (all of which scarred him, took some vital piece of him—I needed him alive, not whole), I saw that he must have some good reason to go on living, for, as I have often reflected, it is a simple thing to give oneself up to the sea. So I gave him an island like mine, not good for much but raising goats and men, and a wife of perfect steadfastness (the mirror image of the woman I knew so long ago).

In retrospect, it is obvious that "Nobody" was a *nom de guerre*, the alias of an anonymous raider. The choice of sobriquet suggests a man infatuated with his own cleverness. He carried himself like a warrior, but preferred getting me drunk to attacking me openly. His mind, I thought, must be like a city of a thousand twists and turns, founded on deceit, with never an open line of sight or a straight passage. Fluent in lies, he must have been the death of many men greater than himself. And he was loyal to his men, or so I liked to think, as it increased my pleasure in making monsters pluck them from his ships while he stood by helplessly, and in making their ghosts weep for burial.

The island farmers are less timid now that I am blind. They bring me fruit and salted meat and listen with more than polite interest while I tell my stories. Some parts of the tale have gelled over the years, though others I improvise or vary as suits the audience's mood or mine—even now it gives me pleasure to invent new sufferings for him. For all that, my bloodthirstiness has lessened—I no longer groan in my sleep or dream of catching him and wrenching out his bones. The ruin where my eye was is not painful anymore, and my days are calm, even joyful. Sometimes I think I am grateful, that sight would be a distraction.

27

NO MAN'S WIFE

In his sojourn in the land of the dead Odysseus saw Penelope among the listless shades. With his broadsword he cleared a path through the muttering ghosts but she receded, seeming not to see him. He called out her name and chased after her, leaving his men behind, catching up with her in a dark glade full of asphodel where she sat at a loom weaving a long shroud. He made to speak to her but, remembering the ways of the dead, used his sword to dig a small pit over which he opened a vein.

She was drawn to the blood and drank, something like light coming into her eyes. "It is no kindness to bring the dead back to themselves. We are wretched but do not know it until you remind us. Why have you come to trouble me, stranger?" she said, looking up from where she knelt in the dust with red streaks on her white face.

"I am a traveler from Troy who has come a long way with Odysseus, your husband," he said. "What cruel fate befell you that the deep-thinking hero must now return to a cold and empty hall?"

"You lie," she said apathetically, "Odysseus is no more. When he had been gone ten years and a little more I went to Delphi to learn what had become of him. I gave the priest a silver bowl embossed with sphinxes that had been part of my dowry. He led me down into a cave dark as a womb where it smelled of wet stone and hot metal. I asked the shuddering oracle, whom I heard but could not see, whether Odysseus would come back to me. 'No man will return to you, but not for a long while,' she said, and all my hope fell to the floor.*

"Back in Ithaca, many men sought my hand. I told them I would marry when I had finished my husband's funeral shroud, and I kept weaving it and weaving it. They grew impatient—they pled and reasoned but were working themselves up to violence.

"I wanted to secure my son's patrimony. So I sent Telemachus off to visit Sparta and when he was gone gave a feast to which I made a point of inviting every man who had courted me. I let it be known that by the end of the feast I would be with the man who would be my husband. The wine was poisoned—painful and slow, but sure. I drank first. And so I made a liar of myself, for

---

*It was a little more than ten years after leaving Ithaca that Odysseus encountered the cyclops Polyphemus and as a *ruse de guerre* said his name was Noman.

though I have searched every vale of the shadowlands I have not found even a rumor of him."

"Would you know your husband? Do you not recognize me, at all?" asked Odysseus gently.

"Yes, I recognize you. You are the living, come with all your heat and blood to trouble my shadows and dust. Traveler, begone from here."

"But I must come back once more when my days are done and then, finally, you will be waiting for me," he said and reached out to touch her cheek but she slipped away like a fish in a stream.

28

PHOENICIAN

Since you ask, I will tell you. So drink your wine and take your ease, traveler. The nights are long in Ithaca and tomorrow will look after itself.[*]

I was born on Limnos, an island far west of here, the last place the sun rises. The farms on Limnos are scattered and the people are taciturn, miserly and dishonest. The king was Tethios, my father, a grim, silent man. Our house was on a white hill on the westernmost point of the island. On the beach the bones of a ruined temple protruded from the sand and I would play among its weathered stones while Nurse watched me.

Nurse was a Phoenician with a face like a blade and a body like an arrow. Now I know that no one would call her desirable but to me she was beautiful. My mother stayed in bed in a darkened room and my father had no

---

[*]The narrator of this story is apparently Eumaios, the swineherd who sheltered Odysseus when he first returned to Ithaca and later helped him kill the suitors. Most likely, Eumaios is telling his story to Odysseus on the eve of the battle.

interest in nursery matters so she and I were left to our own devices. She would sit me on her knee under the oak atop the hill and in her own language tell me stories of her home, Tyre, the island city, where the sea was the moat and the walls so high that hundred-year waves broke on them without wetting the battlements. She told me how Heracles, also called Melquart, had been the slave of a wicked old king who told him to go and sleep among the waves. Heracles threw a great white stone into the sea to be his bed—the wave from the stone drowned the king's subterranean palace, and the stone itself became Tyre's foundation. She told me of the fire roaring in the belly of the idol of Baal, how the priests bound children with cords and cast them into the flame to appease the god's hunger. She told me of the dye-works where women ground the murex,* dripping crimson to the elbows like a coven of murderesses. She loved me as I loved her, I think, and anyway no one else wanted her.

Early one spring, a Phoenician trading ship dropped anchor in our harbor. There was a general air of holiday as everyone on the island went down to see what they had to sell. Nurse was especially excited, as she had not spoken her mother tongue to anyone but me since my father took her for a slave. She stood on the shingle rattling away with the traders while the other women

---

*The Tyrians were famous for the dye they extracted from the red murex, a kind of marine snail.

picked over amber, knives and linen. All smiles, their captain brought her aboard to drink wine. I sat on the sand and heard them laughing.

The next morning she told me to look after myself and hurried off. I followed her at a distance, and saw her go into the woods with the captain. I hid behind an oak and heard her tell him that she was the king of Tyre's daughter, abducted so many years ago, and still homesick. "Tomorrow we go and you should come with us," the captain said. She laughed with pleasure and said she would and she might bring Tethios's most precious treasure with her, for all that it was getting too big to carry.

The next morning when the tide was in the offing the Phoenicians sent a messenger to the court with their goodbyes and a gift for the queen, a necklace of rough gold and amber. While the women passed it from hand to hand, Nurse slipped away and made for the ship. I overtook her not far from the anchorage, and, weeping, asked her how she could bear to leave me. She gave a start and comforted me, smoothing back my hair, explaining that she was leaving me because I was my father's only son and I would miss him. I said I would miss no one but her. So we went on the ship together, and she held my hand and ignored the sailors, who ignored us in turn, as though we were ghosts.

Limnos faded behind us. Nurse took ill and kept to her berth, her face turned away from me. On the fifth day out she stopped speaking and on the sixth she

stopped breathing. She went into the sea with little ceremony, swung over the side by sailors with wooden faces,
her lover among them. They spoke in their own tongue
(not knowing I understood them) of taking me back to
Limnos for ransom, but decided it was too risky, and that
anyway I had some value other than as a king's son. Their
talk of profits cheapened my mourning and it was a relief
when we came to Ithaca and I stepped ashore a slave.

29

INTERMEZZO

We sailed that night from Ilium. Dirty snow on deck, the sizzle of snowflakes dissolving on the swell, the yellow lights of the city dwindling behind me. I spent the night sitting on the prow, the bosun bringing hot wine when the watch changed. We passed in and out of low cloud banks floating on the sea. Distant lights from little coastal towns glittered like myriads of tiny luminous creatures drawn up out of the deep by a rare current.

My life in the East had passed as a dream—it was an unpleasant, even painful time, and already the recollection of it all but eluded me. (In the future it would come to me only in fragments: a small, cramped tent with the lamplight shining on Achilles' obdurate frowning face, the warm glow of his armor, the shadows on the worried faces of his bent crowd of supplicants. The humming of arrows as they darkened the sky above us. The interior of the horse, confined and creaking like the hold of a ship.) I tried to imagine the life awaiting me in Ithaca but as much as I turned my mind toward it I could not see that island's forests, walls, towns or harbors. All that came to mind were a few disconnected images—palm trees in washed-out light, the broken surface of a temple pool, cracked blue tiles, a silver chariot before whitewashed walls. Ithaca, I recall saying, is good for raising men and goats and little else. Ithaca had become a sequence of images that could be made to fit almost anywhere.

I lay listening to the hissing of the bow wave and tried to tell the future. The ship will dock and I will set foot on the wharf for the first time in ten years. I will walk up through the harbor and see my father's father's house standing there on the hill. And what then? Images flickered through my mind. The face of a young woman, her suspicion turning to welcome. The creak of a bowstring. An island far away and bound in darkness, a woman's shadow moving over its hills. I stared up at the lightening sky and imagined that the contours of the bluing intricate clouds, just visible, were a map of the near future.

30

VICTORY LAMENT

My birthrights were great strength, copper beauty and an enduring sadness. My mother Thetis told me I could not die and indeed though the years withered men like autumn leaves I persisted. Just as my body stayed young, so did my temperament—I wandered from Gaul to India and back, taking great delight in seeking out the best fighters and cutting them down. One year a new star appeared in the sky and I decided to go to the imperial court and appropriate its significance for myself before the astrologers arrogated it to flood, locusts or plague. I won an audience with Emperor Agamemnon by thrashing the sixteen spearmen who stood scowling before his summer palace. I sketched the shadow of a bow, smiled up into his darkening countenance and proposed a wager. I would engage his two greatest champions both at once—if they won, I would be his slave and set his perfumed foot on the necks of nations, but if I won I would loot what I liked from his palace. The vizier Odysseus whispered worriedly in His Imperial Highness's ear but Agamemnon brushed him aside, smiled at me hatefully and summoned his paladins—Ajax, built like a mountain, who drew his strength from the deeps of the earth, and Diomedes, who was so fast he moved in a blur and had crossed blades with the gods.

The fight would have been disappointing had there not been the emperor's impotent fury for relish. When I tired of the hollow sound of their skulls knocking together I dumped them before the throne and claimed my rights. I loudly announced that I would start my pillaging in the harem and strode straight past the eunuchs with their cruelly barbed halberds and up the long stairs to the high tower where Agamemnon, ever fearful of cuckolding, kept his women.

I had not meant to do more than provoke him into seeking out the greatest champions to kill me—that way I would know once and for all if I had any equal in the world. Agamemnon lacked invention—it must have been Odysseus who advised him to weld shut the doors to the harem tower that first night while I was distracted. The walls were five feet thick and the windows no wider than arrow slits. There was no way to get to the roof and no way out except the fused iron doors—I was stuck. The girls must have been expensive, as they kept passing in food and water. They were a delight at first, but soon became tiresome—always a hothouse of intrigue and gossip, the harem's suddenly absolute isolation brought out an absolute cattiness. There was nothing to do but practice the sword and meditate, day in and day out.

A year and a day after I had been locked inside the harem there was a shriek of metal and I went down to find them prying open the door to my prison. Odysseus was there holding a white flag of truce. Behind him were fifty men with nets and bolos and a hundred archers with what I could tell even at a hundred paces were poison-tipped arrows. Odysseus apologized for the mixed reception—he had wanted to talk to me but Agamemnon would not permit the gate to be opened without all this, he said, gesturing toward the pale, trembling soldiers behind him. He sat down beside me on the stairs and poured arak from a copper flask. I had not tasted spirits since my confinement and drank happily. Odysseus said he thought that I had come to court not so much for conquest as in hopes of finding a worthy enemy. If this was the case, I was bound to be disappointed—the late Ajax, undefeated prior to his death at my hands, was the strongest the empire had to offer. I could always set myself single-handed against all the emperor's armies but at best that would be like a lion fighting a swarm of biting ants.

He said I had chosen poorly by going to the harem—had I gone to the treasury instead I might have found the secret panel set in the floor that led to a maze of caverns in one of which there was a cedar chest guarded by tiny white spiders (their poison of staggering virulence) and within that chest found what he had brought me today, a small key of black and twisted iron. This was the key, he told me, that opened the gate the gods had locked behind them when they tired of the world and finally left it to its own devices. It had been held close by the Atreides dynasty since time out of mind, as much to keep the gods out as mortals in. Odysseus freely admitted that he wanted me out of the empire but said that the only way to do this was to see that I got what I wanted else-where—he told me to go and seek a match among the gods because I would not find it among men.

I set out for the iron gates of heaven, which as is widely known are a thousand miles north and a thousand miles east of the mountaintop grave of the philosopher Lao Tsu. In time I found them, set in a high glacier on a mountain peak where blizzards never let up shrieking.

I unlocked the great black iron door with Odysseus's key and opened it onto a staircase that led up indefinitely into a still, starry night. I trudged upward for some inde-terminate duration, the night unchanging around me. (I still don't know how long it took. Now and then my mind would turn from the task of putting one foot in front of the other but I pulled myself back from the brink of reflection, knowing it would lead to despair.) At last I reached the top and found a silver gate that was the twin of the iron one, though it had been so long since I left the Earth (it was invisible behind me and had been time out of mind) that I wondered if the first gate had been a dream. I smashed the silver gate with my fist and burst in on an astonished heavenly bureaucracy, blue-skinned ministers of celestial protocol gaping at me from between their desks' towers of memoranda. For all their surprise, retaliation was swift and comprehensive—slavering, white-tusked demons bayed insults and hurled burning brands, a grim-faced god with the Milky Way in his quiver shot stars at me and mad-eyed devas attacked from all sides at once and no side at all, and through it all the Emperor of Heaven for whom the world and all the worlds were as baubles in his hand did not deign to turn his august eyes in my direction. Here, finally, was true power to oppose me but to my lasting sorrow I had forgotten what failure was and my blade flickered through the hearts of my antagonists until I came before the Emperor of Heaven who continued to disdain me even as I cut through his excellent jade neck. He came crashing down from his high throne, mountain ranges wearing away on the distant Earth as he fell and fell and fell. Now I have taken his throne and read his book and the now-docile devas flit about my shoulders, waiting, perhaps forever, for me to impart my wisdom, which is that I have learned nothing, know nothing, wish I had never picked up a sword, left my hut, been born.

ATHENA IN DEATH

An arrow, a reaver, a ship, a wave, a cold swell, a white fog—death was destined to come from the sea for Odysseus Laertides and in the fullness of time it did. He had often meditated on the form it would take and thought he had considered and prepared himself against every seaborne end but in the event dying was confusing, a jumble of impressions of foam and blood and long empty vistas. He was relieved to see that Athena, who had abandoned him for decades and, he had thought, for good, was there to greet him and gather him to her breast (he had never before been this close to her, never touched her—her skin was very hot and she smelled like metal and summer). She grinned at him like she had when they were plotting an especially pernicious piece of mischief and said she had been waiting for him for a long time, poised for the moment when his thread would be cut and she would swoop down from Olympus to catch his soul before it could start the long trip into the dark. The underworld was not for him, not even its Elysium, she said. For Odysseus, her best beloved among mortals, her favorite since he was born, she would, as his final reward, make for him whatever afterlife he wanted.

Odysseus thought a little while (or possibly a long while—he was distantly aware of nights passing, greenery sprouting from oak trees and withering away, through all of which Athena's grin was immovable) and asked to be young again, or at least not old, and to spend eternity making his way from a war indefinitely far in the past to an island indefinitely far in the future. He would remember that the war had been painful, but that he had won it. The details of the island would be vague—splintered images would come from time to time—but he would be certain that it represented the consummation of every desire. He did not want to know that he was a ghost. Let trials and cruel kings and monsters come, he said, and let them all be overcome at the last second. Above all, he said, stay with me this time.* She would, she said, and she had.

Athena granted his request. Moreover, as she knew full well that the age of heroes was fading like an ember, she turned her back on Mount Olympus and went with him.

Much as she dotes on him her mind sometimes wanders and she looks back in on Earth. When this happens

---

*In the standard *Odyssey*, Athena did not speak to Odysseus between his departure from Troy and his arrival back on Ithaca.

a certain comet passes through the constellation Orion for the space of seven days before slipping back out into the great night. My grandfather was privileged to observe this rare celestial phenomenon and averred that his grandfather before him had seen it in his youth.*

---

*This idiosyncratic and oddly personal interjection is the only one of its kind in the *Lost Books*. Otherwise, the narrator does not offer direct commentary in those stories told in the third person.

32

STONE GARDEN

When Odysseus was in the land of the dead the veiled ghost of a woman sought him out, the murmuring shades making way for her. The beauty of her eyes, whose green was just visible through her cloth, was such that Odysseus suffered her to approach and drink from his sacrifice's blood. She said:

> There was a time before I became a gardener when my life was full of noise, children, cousins and most of all suitors, of whom I had many and spurned most. I had a rival, powerful and jealous, and things came to a crisis. Afterwards I retired to tend my island, taking delight only in form, making every tree on the hill, every stone on the beach reflect the harmony of my design. I rejoiced in my garden and had no visitors and was very lonely. Sometimes I thought I heard the footsteps of tentative guests, unsure of their welcome, and my heart quickened. But when I went to meet them

the footsteps stopped, leaving only their echo among the multiplying statues of the garden. I hissed and cried my frustration and the days were long for me.

One day I thought I saw someone walking along my well-tended paths. I went to meet him and found not a visitor or a statue but a silver disc hanging in the air, reflecting the brilliant sun. I stared into it as it floated toward me, unearthly, the moon come down to haunt me. A flash of bronze in my peripheral vision and my mind is full of the distinctive lineaments of a sword.

Suddenly it is twilight. A shadow with a blade and shield stands beside me in the half darkness, insubstantial as smoke. But there is someone else— I turn and see a beardless young man with blond oiled hair. I am delighted—it is my lover from so long ago, so slender and fleet. I reach for his hand, which he gives me willingly. Hermes* says, "I had hoped not to see you again, Medusa."

---

*Lord of snakes and god of ghosts, Hermes was the psychopompos, the god who conducted newly dead souls to the underworld.

33

CASSANDRA'S RULE

Running from her brother through the old city in the early morning when the shadows were sharp and her skin iridescent in the sun she found a refuge in the temple of Apollo. Within, it was dark and cool and the silence was a comfort—she lay down and put her head on her arms, watching the statue of the god, who seemed lost in thought. She fell into that middle sleep where everything is grey stillness and stayed there until the grey coalesced into a beautiful man speaking softly of an island full of cattle whose death would be many men's undoing, of a mother wading in the River Styx and holding her infant son by the heel that would one day blossom into his ruin, of the inexorable tightening of fate's net. She woke up and found Apollo regarding her thoughtfully. He said, "Never mind. No one will ever believe you."

Thereafter, whenever she looked at the sun long enough she could hear Apollo as he talked to himself, a slow, endless monologue touching on all things under his far-reaching gaze, and in that way she knew the future.

With staring, sun-blind eyes she learned the sad ends of Hector her brother and Priam her father and wept for them even as they sat beside her. She begged them to flee, to pray, to stay inside on inauspicious days but they only smiled, kissed her, brushed her aside. She saw that the war that was coming to Troy could not be won, that it could only end in flame and fields sewn with salt, but no one would be persuaded. She heard her own fate, to warn but be disbelieved, to inveigh against the horse as it was pulled through the city gates, finally to be a slave in a distant country. She thought of fleeing but knew from the fall of the city wall's shadow, from the voice of the wind sighing through the towers and from the shapes of the bright clouds overhead, always changing, that it would not be so, that her fate was elsewhere, that for once the god had lied.

34

PRINCIPIA PELAGICA

The rigging creaks and the bow wave hisses as Homer lies in his hammock looking up at the shadows of ropes crisscrossing the glory of the white sail's glowing spread, the sun behind it. The stories he has been composing float just below the surface of his mind and, blissful, he falls asleep. This is his dream:

> Thin light, driftwood, seawrack, black flies aim-
> lessly circling. No one else was on the beach,
> which surprised me, made me think of the con-
> tour of the continent and how much of the coast,
> at any given time, is empty or nearly empty, of a
> lone fisherman in waders or a spark of campfire
> seen at distance from a high coastal road. Some-
> thing half buried in sand, too angular and regular
> to be kelp. Sweeping away the sand, thinking it
> might be an old chunk of keel or jetsam from the
> off-shore refineries. Instead it is a book, the cover

cut from some thick hide, salt-swollen, pitted and abrasive. The pages are slick, fibrous, plasticine—not paper. I open it at random and there is a page of neatly spaced symbols, about eleven wide and twenty deep. It is no alphabet I recognize—I wonder if it could be Sanskrit or katakana and, briefly, the letters' gestalts twist themselves to my expectations but I see they are different, in fact not letters at all, but tiny, intricate drawings, no two alike. The contour of each symbol is immensely detailed, what looks like a straight line from a distance revealing itself on close inspection as an elegant welter of hooks and curlicues. Study reveals nothing, just intricate enigmatic shapes that could as well be the scars of a burrowing worm as an accounts ledger as a Confucian classic, no visible order beyond the regular spacing and no symbol ever repeating (unless the ink ran into the grain of the page somehow and I am focused on something irrelevant). Having nothing better to do, I turn the pages as the sun slides across the sky and the tide comes in. The breaking waves make a faint blue light (luciferin and luciferase mixing in the oceanic bacteria, a part of my distracted mind notes) by which I read (if that is the word) the book, poring over each page, wearing away the sense of entropy. Now there is an intuition, an intimation of order, though when I rally myself to articulate it, nothing comes. If I can't put it into words is it real? I wonder. Night now, headlights sliding over high distant coastal cliffs.

EPIGRAPH

There is a silence in desolate places that is terrible for a man too long away from home and it was waiting for Odysseus in Ithaca Town. No human voices there, no smoke of fires, no creak of wagons. Grass grew in the street and a thin, feral cow regarded him suspiciously while browsing on deadfalls in a fig orchard. The master mariner thought, "Caution. Who knows what mischief befell this town and what mischief is left? After all these years coming back don't go rushing in like a puppy." So he left the road and went up onto a hill overlooking the town, concealed himself among the trees next to a hut that had once been the swineherd's and settled in to watch. All afternoon there was only stillness and birdsong and several times he caught himself dozing.

Night fell. A bright, full moon rose and illuminated the flawless, static island. There was not even a breath of wind. In the night's last hours Odysseus stole down through the trees toward his house. Irresistibly reminded of his night-time forays into Troy, where at least there had been a friendly army to retreat to, he slipped through the open-hanging gate of his courtyard, hand on the hilt of his sword.

Within, nothing. Moss on the dung-heap and disintegrating potsherds. A dog's verdigrised brass collar clanked underfoot. The house was cold and still. As he crept down a corridor, he looked back, saw his footprints in the dust and desiccated leaves, and discarded stealth.

Odysseus murmured to himself, "There are only so many possibilities. The town could have been wiped out in an attack. There could have been a mass emigration—to avoid raiders, for instance. There could have been a sickness. Each of these possibilities entails certain signs. Every event is the cause of myriad effects and it is effectively impossible that a disaster of this magnitude could have swept all the people away and left no record of the manner of their passing. The world is a fundamentally orderly place, never impervious to reason. I will look until I find this record and read it and know what came to pass here."

He searched the house in earnest for the marks of recent history. In one storeroom he found an amphora of sweet wine he thought he had laid down himself. In another he found a cobwebbed pile of weapons and armor. Altogether, he found:

an orange coral hairpin
a broken loom

an empty, undecorated quiver

a broken stick of incense, still fragrant when he
turned it in his fingers

a clay washbasin

He went into the dimness of the great hall. It was
a wreck—tables overturned and broken, shattered bowls,
a foot-bath. He kicked an ancient, desiccated cow's hoof.
Arrows stuck in the wall here and there, but when he
tried to pull them out they crumbled. The aftermath of a
battle? The shafts were embedded in just one wall—an
archery contest? Idle vandals? He found his great bronze
bow lying under some chairs, streaked with green but as
strong and supple as ever. This he kept, having missed it
many times on the field at Troy and in his wandering.

He left the house and walked among the outbuildings.
The sky was beginning to glow. Ropes were strung between the roof of the roundhouse and the corral.* The
garden was in a sad state of neglect and the fences were
falling down. He resisted an impulse to forget his search
and start setting things right.

The sun rose and in the forgiving early light he could
almost pretend that his house was not abandoned but still
a living place. He went into the cellar, which he had

---

*This is where the maids who had lain with the suitors were hanged to death by
Odysseus, Eumaios and Telemachus after the suitors' slaughter in the standard version of the *Odyssey*.

been postponing. Picking his way over toppled, broken jars, he found an intact iron-bound chest shoved into a corner. At last, an answer. He forced the lock with his sword. Within the chest were a funeral shroud, belt buckles, a length of fine linen, and a sack of bronze nails.

That morning he found an abandoned boat and left the island, swearing to come back one day with answers.

36

A MOTE IN
OCEANIC DARKNESS

Waterlogged, frozen, exhausted, Odysseus clung to a floating spar, dark waves surging over him. He could not help but think that this was happening to someone else, that someone, a stranger, was being consumed by the sea, was near drowning. His teeth had long since stopped chattering when a were-light appeared on the waters and his mind went from pain and dullness to clarity—Pallas Athena was with him. He said, Goddess, who are you, to find me and bear me up when I am lost in the waste? In the sudden stillness she said:

Water flowing through pipes, pouring into unlit reservoirs there to eddy in silence. Runes of ephemeral fire. A book of many pages written in inks that vanish and reappear. A twilight forest haunted by beasts, watchful and inquisitive. Steadfast of heroes. An onion, an ocean, a palimpsest, a staccato machine of oiled iron gears. These are

among the metaphors with which I describe myself, like a hand trying to grasp itself by reaching
into a mirror.

37

ATHENA'S WEAVE

Midnight came and still Odysseus lay awake, in his own house again after twenty years. He lay under a pile of sheepskins in the portico, his gaze traveling round and round the once familiar walls as though they held some secret, the answer to his agony. He had come a long way to get there only to find his home had become an enemy camp and for a moment his heart failed him. Courage, he told himself—the cyclops, whose rage was like an avalanche, was worse than this. These are but men—boys, really—none of them seasoned in war, no three of whom I could not cut down in seconds, but there are close on fifty of them. How shall I kill them when I am only one? He wanted to walk past the suitors where they slept in the main hall and go to his own bed but knew it would be the death of him. Eventually his tears dried and he drifted close to sleep.

In the grey middle ground between dream and waking Athena appeared to him as she sometimes did and said, "Do not fear, wanderer. There could be fifty times fifty men such as these all baying for your blood and still you would triumph. Like me, you have the knack of stringing victory together out of whatever is at hand." Odysseus replied, "It is a shame that the way of the Olympians is to help their protégés help themselves—if I thought you would slaughter them all for me I would indeed rest at ease. If you wish to do so, please proceed— do not stand on ceremony with so old a friend as me." Athena laughed and went back to Olympus, but before she went she gave him a dream.

There was a sense of movement and of distant women whispering and Odysseus found a cloth in his hands which he immediately knew was the weave of fate. Its manifold complexities drew his eyes but Athena whispered in his ear not to be distracted, to look for the bright, strong thread of his own life, how it was interwoven with the threads of his wife and son, Menelaus and Helen, all the Trojans, Calypso and Circe, the isle of Ithaca. The suitors' fates were slight things, just barely bound to the world. Myriad futures opened up before them but all were short and all ended bitter.

Odysseus woke bemused, feeling like a seer. He floated gracefully through the deception of the household,* watching himself as though he were an actor in a theater, immersing himself in the role of wandering beggar and studying his enemies with clear eyes. When

---

*Recall that Odysseus returned to his house posing as a beggar.

things came to a head and the bronze bow was strung* he fired one arrow after another into the suitors' chests with the utmost detachment—he had a vision of standing in the dewy corral in the hills above the house, streaming sweat in the late morning sun, sending arrow after arrow into the bole of the oak a hundred paces distant. Each time he nocked an arrow he could smell the wet grass and see the sun burning behind the oak leaves.

When the remaining suitors managed to arm themselves and come to close quarters there was none of the usual rush of battle. A man would rush up waving a sword, present an opening into which Odysseus put his blade, fall down dead and so on, one after another.

After the tears of reunion dried and his and Penelope's joy had reached a less fevered pitch, she showed him the shroud she had been weaving for his father, Laertes. Odysseus picked up the ordinary and unfateful piece of cloth and recognized the fabric shown him by Athena, the improviser, the deceiver.

---

*With the connivance of his son Telemachus, Odysseus had the suitors try to string his massive bronze bow. As a joke the suitors gave the beggar a try, and were thereby undone.

38

THE LONG WAY BACK

In retrospect Theseus saw it was Daedalus he should have feared. Minos was just a king, however wise, and Ariadne just a girl, however beautiful, but neither Daedalus's cunning nor his labyrinth had any end. Theseus had come to Crete as a young man, nominally a prisoner and a sacrifice but laughing in his heart and out for blood. He was not yet old enough to believe in death, though he had already killed a dozen men. Watching their lives' blood stain his spear and hands had only taught him that death is the province of others.

In their white robes of hieratic office King Minos and his golden-haired daughter Ariadne greeted the Athenian offerings as they disembarked in Knossos port. Theseus, the Athenian captain, considered it charming to treat his enemy with great politeness and replied to their official greeting with the utmost courtesy. Minos, a fair-minded man, told them at length why they were going to die. He

spoke of Pasiphaë* and monstrous couplings, white cattle
flying across the sea and crazed hatred in divine eyes. Theseus barely listened—they were where they were and it
didn't matter much how they got there, and anyway he
was distracted by Ariadne, who first avoided but soon
returned his gaze. After Minos's speech the Athenians were
led away to the opulent cells where they would be kept for
a week before being sent into the labyrinth—the Minotaur
preferred victims healthy, well fed and free of disease.

On the second night they were taken to a banquet
served in the balconies overlooking an arena; below
them, slaves leapt over charging bulls and initiates danced
with double-headed axes. The old engineer Daedalus
was there, wearing a white, plain, food-stained robe and
ignoring both his companions and the ceremonies below,
all his interest absorbed by the diagrams he was drawing
on the table with the lees of the wine. Beside him, a
bare-breasted matron with an ageless face and hard smile
made vain and persistent attempts at conversation (which
made Theseus smile—her accoutrement was outrageous
by Athenian standards but her face and manner reminded
him of his mother). Minos made several toasts to Dae-

---

*Pasiphaë was Minos's wife. She had offended the goddess Hera, who punished
her with a great passion for a sacred white bull. Daedalus built a sort of hollow
cow simulacrum for her, with which she was able to consummate her desire. The
issue of that union was the Minotaur, a cannibalistic monster half man and half
bull.

dalus, who received them with forced good grace—rumor had it he was an unwilling guest in Crete. Minos extolled Daedalus's many achievements—not only had he designed and built the labyrinth at the heart of the palace but also the palace itself and the city with its harbors, fanes, libraries and universities. He had even laid out the farms, fields and roads around Knossos, not to mention his architectural projects in the outlying provinces, the mainland and even the Lydian and Persian kingdoms far to the east. Theseus thought that he did not look like much for someone who exceeded all men in the scope of his achievements. With his thin neck, long nose and heavy grizzled head, the only remarkable things about him were his abstractedness and the intensity with which he regarded his vinous sketches. Ariadne excused herself to check on her Athenian guests—she stood by Theseus's chair and he thanked her for her hospitality, touching her hand for emphasis.

The next night Ariadne visited Theseus on the pretext of expounding her father's justice, the necessity of keeping the sacred monster placated, the reasonable and traditional subjugation of Athens to Knossos. He made every pretense of attentiveness and sat close enough that their legs were touching. Things proceeded. She was not his first lover but the danger, the secrecy and the promise of bloodshed gave the affair a luminous intensity he had known before only in battle. She loved him, loved him completely, more than her parents, her temple or her life, she said in a thick, clotted voice, her white face red with emotion. She left for a while and came back with the wherewithal for victory—a thick ball of twine, a sharp sword and the key to his cell.

When Ariadne had gone, Theseus crouched by his door for some indefinite duration, listening, hearing nothing. When impatience finally overcame caution, he slipped out of his cell and followed Ariadne's directions through torch-lit corridors and down dark stairs. He padded along barefoot, trading comfort (the floor was very cold) for silence, prepared to bluff then kill anyone he met, but he did not see another soul on his way to the labyrinth's door. Ariadne had told him that it would not be locked—all who wished to enter were free to do so. He tied one end of his twine to a torch bracket, drew his sword and crept in, his blood singing a war-song.

Within were passages, arcades and high galleries all wrought of the same blank white stone, echoes caroming at random through the interlocking rooms and interlaced corridors, tortuously returning the soft slap of his foot-steps. Sometimes he thought he heard the beast moaning and sighing in its sleep; the frisson made him bare his teeth. Mastering himself, Theseus reflected that these sounds were not so ominous; if it was asleep, like any man or animal, then the creature could not be an immortal with ichor in its veins and eyes wide for a thousand-year watch.* Furthermore, it was accustomed to killing terrified children, not an armed and determined warrior (though he was only sixteen, he merited the name).

From the layout of the palace he had inferred the rough dimensions of the labyrinth but either he had been wrong or got lost because he wandered through more corridors than he had thought the labyrinth could hold. As he went deeper, it appeared that Daedalus sometimes used the labyrinth as a workshop—in some rooms there were relief maps of Knossos carved into the walls, sometimes with notes in a spidery hand about strategic weak points and the relative merits of mangonels versus arbalests on wharves, walls, promontories and towers. In other rooms he found drawings of birds and sea creatures (some of the drawings remarkably life-like, others of carefully posed skeletons), waxy yellow crystals in numbered boxes and a shelf of books all of whose pages were parchment-thin mirrors with varying degrees of warp and translucency. In one room he discovered a map of the labyrinth but it was difficult to associate it with his recollections of the passages he had seen and he soon found other chambers with other maps, equally convincing and on inspection wholly contradictory.

He found the Minotaur sleeping in an arcade, flat on

*A reference to Argos, a thousand-eyed giant employed by Hera as the guardian of a grove of golden apples. His eyes slept independently—no matter the time of day or night, hundreds would be awake and looking in any given direction.

his back (he was innocent of clothing and evidently male), his huge limbs sprawled out around him. The creature was big—upright he would have been around seven feet tall, Theseus guessed. The Minotaur's horns were long and sharp enough to skewer a man but Theseus was nevertheless relieved—in his imagination the monster had snorted fire and filled a cavern with its bulk, but now that he saw the beast he recognized him as just another victim. Theseus crept forward, surprised that the creature could sleep through his heart's clamor. He raised his sword to strike the carotid, but hesitated at the thought of killing a sleeping foe—he was still half a boy and loved honor.

In that moment the Minotaur woke and swatted him away with a massive paw. Theseus recovered and sprang to his feet as the Minotaur bellowed and charged with lowered horns. Theseus feinted left and stepped right, as he had practiced so many times with his father's bulls in Athens, and as the beast went roaring by he cut through its spine at the base of its neck. The Minotaur slowed, then teetered and fell heavily, comically, landing on its stomach with a loud slap. A blood bubble formed on its nostril, burst, and then stillness. Dead, the monster was pitiful, its glazed cow eyes full of terror. Theseus ineffectually tried to clean his sword on the walls (he did not want to sully his shirt and could not bear to approach the corpse), regarded his fallen enemy for a moment, and turned to trace his way back out of the labyrinth. It occurred to him to gather up the twine but it would have been hard to re-roll and anyway he thought, "Let them see the artifice by which their god was killed by Theseus the Athenian."

Outside the labyrinth Ariadne was waiting for him. Her cheeks were tear-stained but she greeted him with composure. They plucked the other Athenians out of their cells and stole away to the docks where they waved torches in the damp night air and their ship, which had been cruising outside the harbor every night, came in to fetch them. Once they were well out to sea they stopped creeping around the deck and speaking in whispers and started laughing, shaking their fists at King Minos and the city whose tutelary demigod Theseus had just butchered. Now and then they fell silent and there were no sounds but the rippling of the sails and the murmur of the bow wave. After a while someone would say, "Steak, anyone?" and the laughter would begin again. Ariadne did not participate, but Theseus held her hand and kissed her and told her how beautiful Athens was.

When they arrived, King Aegeus embraced Theseus and welcomed Ariadne with the courtesy due a princess and the warmth due a daughter. She and Theseus were married on the Acropolis under a hunter's moon while the people waved torches and sang. Their first son was conceived that night and not long after old Aegeus privately told Theseus that he was replete with honor and intended to abdicate so that he, Theseus, could enjoy the kingship while he was young. One son was born and then another and Theseus settled into maturity, the wise king of a prosperous people.

One summer many years later, when Ariadne's golden hair was turning silver, Theseus returned from a hunt and realized that it was the day the sacrifices would have gone to Crete. He thought of his fight with the Minotaur, and on a nostalgic impulse went down into the cellars beneath the castle to look for Ariadne's sword. The cellars, excavated centuries before as a refuge against invaders, were dim, extensive and confusing. He lost his way but kept walking through the low corridors, taking turns at random, sure he would soon find his bearings. In this he was proved correct when he turned a corner and came upon a length of twine laid along the floor, disappearing down the hall in both directions. Beside it lay the sword he had been looking for. He picked up the blade, chose a direction and wonderingly followed the twine until he emerged from the labyrinth in Knossos to find Ariadne there waiting for him, golden-haired, a girl, calm and composed, her cheeks wet with tears.

Once again he went through the motions of escape but this time his heart was not in it. He distrusted Ariadne, thinking she must be in league with Daedalus and Minos, trying to break him with her sorcery, tricking him into a labyrinth without boundaries. On the boat she went to him for comfort, but he was cold to her and she soon went off to sit by herself—the other Athenians took Theseus's cue and ignored her. Theseus watched her with hard eyes and the next day announced that he needed to unship ballast and ordered the ship to Naxos. He did not force her from the ship at sword's point, but said he would do so if he had to, even though the only sword he had was the one she had given him and thus probably cursed. She wailed and tried to cling to him but his face did not change as he flicked her tears from his hands and at last she allowed herself to be lowered into the shallows, racked by sobs. He made sail as she waded ashore through the breakers. Later, he thought she must have cursed him and made him forgetful, she who was a priestess and had the ear of spirits, because in his self-absorption he forgot to hoist the white sails and in the moment of his return became a patricide.*

Once the ship was out of sight, Ariadne gave herself over to hysterical weeping and hatred for the man for whom she had betrayed her family and her kingdom. When she had recovered herself enough to breathe and walk again, she climbed to the peak of Naxos's single mountain and made herself a bower in the woods. From time to time a ship would stop to take on water, sometimes even one belonging to her father, but she considered all ties cut and hid until they left. She practiced the

---

*Aegeus, his father, had told the ship's crew to hoist white sails if Theseus lived and black if he had perished. When he saw his son's black-sailed ship sailing toward Athens he flung himself from the Acropolis in despair.

black arts in which she had been instructed since she was a little girl and as years passed turned witchy and potent. Rumors spread of a white nymph haunting Naxos, as beautiful as she was fell and wholly without pity.

She had been lonely for so long she could not conceive of its absence when the stranger washed up on her shore. His lips were blue and his hair matted and tangled with seaweed but in her eyes he was beautiful. She wondered if the half-drowned man would relieve her solitude but she concealed her need even as she nursed him. When he woke she said her name was Concealer* and that he was lucky to be alive. He made all the necessary noises of gratitude but within minutes betrayed her, telling some tale of a distant war and a longed-for home, a son and even a wife awaiting his return. This was painful, but she had learned patience. She gave him the run of the island and said he should go home if he could, she had done all that was in her power to do. He spent his days on the beaches in hopes of seeing a ship but the white fog she had summoned hid everything. On the fourth night she was not surprised, and thus easily able to conceal her delight, when he came to her bed.

As for Theseus, he is in Hell now, wandering and restless, but he is the happiest of shades, always expecting to find himself once again among the blank white halls, the arcades and the high galleries.

---

*The Greek word for concealer is *Calypso*.

39

OCEAN'S DISC

His days were bound by the disc of ocean. In the morning he climbed to the top of her island and sat clutching his knees to his chest against the wind, scanning the horizon for white sails. She left him alone while the sun shone but at dusk she approached out of the gloom, touched his face, took his hand and made to draw him back toward her cave. He pushed her roughly away. "Stay, then," she said, "and look for ships in the dark." He stiffened and turned his back. Her face fell and she said she was sorry, she had not meant it, but there was not much good in keeping watch at night. Carefully nursing his pride, she drew him back to her bed.

In the fading light Hermes watched them go, exasperated. The sharp axe winked in the grass where he had put it weeks ago, the blade carefully turned to catch the evening sun. Behind it was a stand of straight, tall young pines, perfect for ship-building.

SANATORIUM

The war had been long and terrible. Of that Mr. O* was sure, though he could only remember a few disconnected, disconcerting images: Dust hanging over a battlefield, glowing as the sun rose behind it. A brass helmet struck into two pieces. A black tree in the middle of a white plain. Later he was told that these were images from famous songs, emblematic of the war—they had won prizes—and he had almost certainly not seen them firsthand. Nevertheless, he was sure he had been in the war. That was what the nurses told him, or at least implied, and then there were his scars, and why was he in this sanatorium if not to recover? Its small white cubical buildings clung to the island's vertiginous cliffs like swallows' nests, steep stairways tracing parabolic arcs between them. Cats sprawled on the walls tracking the sun and

---

*The text for this chapter omits Odysseus's name, providing instead what is, most probably, the uninflected masculine honorific followed by the letter Omega. "Mr. O" is a reasonably close rendering.

looking skeptically at the azure sea and the ospreys nesting in the parapets. Inexplicably, he wanted to leave. He exhorted himself to show a grateful spirit but this only made him more fretful. He took to plucking threads from his robe in the morning and to rolling bread pills at dinner.*

The days passed like a flock of white birds wheeling overhead and he remembered no more of himself though he frequently resolved to make it his business to do so. Sometimes he found notes he had written to himself that set out meticulous plans for recollection—meditation and a diary, for instance, both of which he had soon abandoned. There was a cedar chest full of keepsakes at the foot of his bed—a bag of salt, a ball of beeswax, a fire-sharpened olive-wood staff, a black-fletched arrow with a black shaft. He took to handling them in hopes of jarring loose a recollection.

During a musical evening a woman in a long green

---

*Around the first millennium B.C., the greatest centers of medical learning in the Greek world were the temples of Asclepius in the Cycladic archipelago. These temples were, in effect, hospitals. At the top of the temple hierarchy were the doctors, of whom each temple had only a few. They were believed to have the ear of the god and supernatural powers of healing. Access to them was carefully restricted—the sick might have to wait in the temple a year and slaughter a hecatomb of livestock before being granted an appointment. Whether this was due to the number of patients, demanding religious practices or a stage-craft of self-importance is not entirely evident from the textual and archaeological records.

The nursing at the temple was carried out by women serving two-year terms in the service of the god. Many women joined after their husbands died. Though they were not exactly nuns, they were celibate for the term of their service and lived an essentially monastic life.

dress sang songs about an old war in which all-but-forgotten heroes fought and died for ends that even they, it seemed, held contemptible. Her plangent voice filled the music room, with its many rows of polite auditors and its ceiling painted like an evening sky. While others applauded, Mr. O reached absently into his coat pocket and found a worn, water-stained note, possibly in his own handwriting, advising him to take the cure with one or the other of the sanatorium's eminent physicians.

He was rapidly granted appointments, with none of the usual sacrifices or purifications. First he went to Dr. Sylvia's rooms in which wide panoramic windows opened over a long drop to the sea, where waves dashed against rock and swordfish were breaching. She spoke to him of the accumulations of moribund memory keeping him uncomfortably and pathologically anchored in the past, and how they could be expunged.

Next he saw Dr. Karidis, whose rooms were down many long flights of stairs, deep within the island, below the level of the sea. They were cool and dark, her silhouette barely visible, her bookshelves no more than conjectures in the shadows. She promised to usher him down and down, away from the moment, away from illness, through the watchful layers of ego, through the restive layer that always dreams and the torpid one that keeps the heart beating, till he need not come up again.

After the consultations he kept to his room for days, refusing to open the door no matter how the nurse knocked, but even without her patient, gentle remonstrances he knew he would have to choose one of them.

He chose Sylvia, explaining to the nurse on the way to the appointment his many and nuanced reasons for doing so, though really it was because she was slightly the less terrible of the two.

The appointment itself was a blank, as were the days that followed.

When he came back to himself he was disoriented and forgetful and explored his room as though it were new to him. There was little to find—a new diary, the pages uncut, and an empty cedar chest. He was going to give up and go back to bed but something moved within him and he kept searching, replying with feigned cheerfulness when a nurse called out from the hall to ask him how he did. His persistence was rewarded with the discovery of a small paper parcel wedged between the mattress and the headboard. Unfolding the paper, he found it bore a drawing of a horse, composed of just a few lines but executed in a confident, energetic hand. Within the paper was a plait of red hair. He held it to his face and inhaled, and a great longing swept over him to which he could not put a name.

One morning soon after, a nurse came to his room, with his draft, he thought, but instead she looked very grave and explained that things had changed. The war, which had been thought to have settled, had only been hesitating. It was racing southward now, scattering all before it, and they had to go. Where will you take me? Mr. O asked. And what about my condition? My consultations? An awkward pause. Resources were limited, the nurse explained, and the rigor of the times such that some, the infirm, the less useful, must be left behind.

To that he had nothing to say. He took to wandering among the white buildings, now empty. Sometimes there was a vague idea of another island, like this one but less lovely and more remote, but he could not put a name to it or remember the way.

41

FIREWORKS

Odysseus roamed wild through the low hills of Ithaca. He swam like an otter through the rough surf and riptides, and knew every cave, thicket, and droning, butterfly-haunted field. He hunted birds in the wood, lying in wait for hours till the silence seemed to fill him (but never a perfect silence—there was always something that was not quite a noise, right at the edge of hearing). The outer world was fog coming in over the ocean, a white sail on the horizon and the rumor of distant relatives. His parents tried to civilize him, and though he learned how to play the lyre and use a sword he saw these as mere formal observances, not touching his real self or the continuity of his days.

In a wood by the sea there was a crumbling Egyptian temple,* its surviving columns carved with men who had

---

*The Eighteenth Nile Dynasty of Egypt had an expansionary phase in pre-Classical times and planted colonies on many islands in the Mediterranean. These flourished briefly but ultimately withered due to a lack of support from Egypt, which was racked by a sequence of civil wars. By the time of the Trojan War only ruins and the occasional place name survived.

the heads of birds and animals—ibis, lion, jackal, hawk, bull. He offered these found gods birds' eggs and arrowheads, and wondered if they had stayed or gone away over the sea.

When the sun was setting he would climb a tree, stretch out along a branch and watch the stars emerge from the deepening blue. Every night, he thought, they were a little closer, falling toward the world so slowly, from so very far away. He would fix a star in his gaze, shut his eyes and then look again, hoping to catch its brightness growing.

✦

Time hissed by like the black arrows whose shadows darkened the plain before Troy. The clutch of the battle was so dense that the soldiers could barely move, constrained on all sides by friend and enemy alike, the bodies of their neighbors bearing them up and weighing them down. The wind lifted waves of white dust that coated faces, swords and armor. When the pressure let up the bleached soldiers dealt each other vicious, clumsy, short-armed blows; the crimson flows and spatters of blood were vivid on their whiteness. When the wind was low Odysseus could see the walls of Troy, never far away and always out of reach.

✦

The smell of the island had not changed—oak, heat, dust, sea, stone—which heartened Odysseus as his white-

sailed ship dropped anchor. As he walked up the road to
his house for the first time in decades he promised himself that he would have nothing more to do with the
affairs of gods or men, would go back to his woods and
the stasis of unvarying afternoons. But it seemed that the
tears of reunion had hardly dried before the house was
filled with wailing and he stood before his father's high
funeral pyre with a torch in his hand. Soon thereafter he
held his first grandchild, and under all the weight of birth
and death a dam somewhere gave way and time flooded
over him. Soon his grandson was tall and strong, as was
the tree over his father's grave, and well before he was
ready he could neither string his great bronze bow, nor
remember the names of the men who had died for him
at Troy, nor speak.

✦

Telemachus, Penelope and the maids carry Odysseus
through the early morning fog to a small building in the
hills behind the house. He has not been conscious for
days and every breath is a violent, shuddering labor. His
hands twitch, briefly, as though in unquiet dreams. The
women fill the pitcher, make the bed and open the windows, leaving Telemachus to stand over his father.

Odysseus is aware of his son standing next to him,
occasionally wiping his forehead, murmuring distractedly
and looking out the window. Somewhere women talk in
low, calm voices. It has been four days since he opened

his eyes, but suddenly, emerging from confusion, he is looking at himself lying in bed. What he had thought were nurses are priests, Egyptians, moving around the room (its stone walls layered in hieroglyphics) making ready knives of black glass and alabaster jars. Next to him stands a jackal-headed man with his arms folded, waiting patiently. "Will they never be done and leave me in peace?" he wonders. And then (after the priests have set the jars by his feet next to a pile of linen bandages and jackal-head has whispered in his ear about immortality) he is lying on a table amid green, rolling hills (it occurs to him that this is like the view from his window, or what it will be in a thousand years when the city has eroded away). The hills envelop him, the valley deepening. The tracks of the wind in the tall grasses. Then it is night, the hills are gone. The table lies in a warm, shallow, unmoving sea. It is perfectly silent (except now and then a distant intimation of worried voices). There is no moon. The stars are dim, as though behind a layer of high clouds. But now they are approaching, and are brighter. Now brilliant. Fireworks.

42

RECORD OF A GAME*

We look at a chess set and see a medieval king, some thin-blooded English Henry sitting in state next to his wanton termagant sorceress wife. Flanking them are machiavel abbés with thin upper lips, all masters of casuistry, elegant courtiers and confirmed atheists. To either side of the cathedral doors (in the checkered board we see first the elongated black-and-white cruciform of a cathedral's floor plan and then the meticulously delimited plantations of a feudal estate) knights stand guard with hands resting on the pommels of zweihänders, plate mail gleaming. At the edges of the kingdom castellans stroll through winter and summer palaces, pulling white sheets from century-old furniture and airing tower bedrooms in preparation for a royal visit. Originally built as fortifica-

*Though written in credible Homeric Greek, the contents of this chapter cannot be dated much before the early Middle Ages. We can assume it is a late addition to the papyrus; in any event, it is the least intact of the papyrus's texts—water damage has made many words and in some cases whole paragraphs matters of inference and conjecture.

tions (with arrow slits and battlements to prove it), the palaces are now country châteaux, their portcullises overgrown with the vines of grapes and tiny, aromatic roses. Hardly worth a mention are the serfs who tend to their betters and their betters' gardens—brave fellows, always ready to drop teapots and shears to take up long pikes for a headlong charge at the enemy.

If our discernment were keener, we would see an altogether more ancient and chaotic battlefield. Four-handed chatarang, the progenitor of modern chess, was created in India for the soldier castes two millennia before Christ with pieces that are, in some cases, hardly recognizable. The queen, now the terror of the board, was then a politic vizier who hovered by the king's side as though fearful of offending. The bishops were war elephants, tusked monsters trampling infantry while the mahouts on their backs shot sling stones and spears. The knights were a cavalry of mounted archers (in the centuries before the stirrup was invented there were no lances), striking swiftly and galloping away. The rooks were not fortresses but war chariots, terrible weapons racing over the battlefield pell-mell, rattling over stones and corpses, wheel-mounted scythes slashing through the legs of men and horses.

The Katishya caste, who were the warriors and rulers of Indian society at the time, believed deeply in the innate elegance of rectilinear order. Their image of paradise was a perfectly level green field bisected north to south by one cold, blue river and east to west by another. Their gardens matched this ideal as closely as possible and, perversely, so did their maps. It was considered self-evident that the earth, an emanation of the mind of god, was arranged in arrays of adjacent, geometrically perfect squares—the failure of the observed geographical world to match this mathematical ideal was easily accounted for by the sinfulness of man and the decadence of the times. The Katishyas' military science resembled their gardening and their cartography—a small repertoire of battlefield maneuvers was drilled into troops and petty officers until they could be executed with repeatable precision, and the mastery of this lexicon and its combinatorics was considered the essence of generalship. The Katishyas considered it the epitome of strategy to take the dust-shrouded confusion of the battlefield and reduce it to a set of symbols on a grid from which could be derived a concise sequence of moves leading inevitably to victory.

Chatarang radiated out from the subcontinent and begat many descendants—it is said that there are as many variations of chess as there are Indo-European languages. Not least among its issue was a game immensely popular in the Achaean societies of the Attic peninsula and the culturally similar islands of the Cyclades in the thirteenth century before Christ. The sum total of the source material for the Achaean variant consists of two complete and three partial game sets (all but one of which were excavated on Chios, known for producing the greatest chess masters), a reference in Hesiod and a primer that was a sort of rarefied transcript of a particularly long and difficult game.

Unlike the ancient, mellow and caste-bound Indian culture in which chatarang originated, the Achaeans were, as a society, desperately concerned with the preeminence of the individual. This difference is reflected in their chess—in the original chatarang, the pieces represent types, interchangeable atoms of abstract ordnance, while in the Achaean game they are individual warriors with names, histories and idiosyncracies.

The Achaean chess primer was the record of a single long game that was believed to embody all that could usefully be said on the subject of chess. On Chios, journeymen who sought their chess master's robes were required to recite the primer in its entirety before a panel of judges who would neither miss nor forgive the slightest error. In its earliest phase, the primer was a raw transcript of move, counter-move and counter's counter, with little or no analysis or exposition. Occasionally, fragments of other classic games were given as a kind of aside, presumably to illustrate some principle of play, though to modern readers their significance can be obscure.

The purity of the primer eroded over time—formulaic descriptions were added as *aides-mémoire* (pieces were called swift-moving, versatile, valuable in the middle game, and so forth), and, most likely, to give the reciter a respite while he gathered his thoughts. Over the centuries, tactical commentary crept into what had once been a purely descriptive account.

By the eighth century B.C. the instructional character of the primer had largely atrophied and the recitation of the by then baroquely ornamented text had become an end in itself. From this time on, the manual, known as the *Iliad*, assumed an essentially literary character, although its original nature was still sometimes discernible in, say, its fixation on the exchange of casualties—Alpha slew Beta with this spear and Gamma slew Alpha with that stone and so on, a meaningless list of deaths unless one knows how to read it as a nuanced sequence of middle-game exchanges. Similarly, the Catalog of Ships* can be usefully read as a treatise on positional play in the opening.

Although the book became more complex over time, the pieces retained a characteristic geometric simplicity. Achilles is represented as a tall, spare warrior holding a shield and a spear, and carved, by preference, from white coral. Nestor is a stooped warrior with two parallel lines incised in the forehead of an otherwise featureless oval face. The stylistic exception is Odysseus, who is always depicted with a detailed, naturalistic countenance that suggests more self-awareness and humanity than the smooth, geometrically regular faces of his peers.

---

*The Catalog of Ships is a section of the second book of the *Iliad* which consists almost entirely of a list of which cities sent how many ships to Troy.

There is a second and most likely apocryphal manual of Achaean chess, the record of a long and bitter endgame played out on a board nearly stripped of pieces. It is even more difficult to associate this book with the practice of chess than the *Iliad*, probably due to the corruption of the text and many late interpolations. It has been speculated that the *Odyssey* is a sort of fantastic parody of a chess book, a treatise on tactics to be used after the game has ended and the board been abandoned by the players, the pieces left finally to their own devices and to entropy. One of the few surviving pieces is Odysseus, inching across the crumbling board toward his home square.

43

ALEXANDER'S ODYSSEY

The instant the prow of his ship touched the shore, Achilles drew back his arm and cast his spear at the high walls of Troy," recited Alexander as his ship ground on the sand and he cast his own spear in the same trajectory toward Troy's crumbling ruins.* His Macedonians jumped down into the breakers, delighted to finally bring war to the empire on whose motions they and their fathers had for so long kept a weather eye.† That evening, Alexander and Hephaestion‡ raced around the tumulus of Achilles' tomb, after which an augur crowned them with laurels and declared that they were Achilles and Patroclus reborn.

---

*Alexander the Great, king of Macedon, is reciting a verse from book seventeen of the *Iliad*, a copy of which he kept under his pillow.

†In 334 B.C. Alexander invaded and conquered the vast, tottering Persian Empire. The Greek world, which had long considered Persia a threat, saw Alexander's invasion as a reprise of the Trojan War, which was, at that point, nearly a millennium past.

‡Alexander's best friend and right-hand man.

Dawn came to the long valley of Gaugamela. A warm band of light burgeoned on the western mountains and spread east, first illuminating an empty expanse of cracked mud and dry grass, then the tents of the Macedonian army, and blinding, for a few moments, the eyes of its sentries. The light poured across no man's land and then over the sprawling Persian host, gleaming red on their helmets, spearpoints, mail and buckles as though on the molten surface of a restless sea. They had been standing in battle array since sunset, their sleepless emperor determined not to be taken unawares. His multitudes blinked uneasily as the sun rose behind them.

By this time most of the Macedonian soldiers had been astir for hours despite the order that everyone get a full night's sleep. They lingered in their tents, lying on their beds with their eyes fixed on nothing, talking quietly with their tent-mates of distant farms, old summers, and what the day might bring.

The pacing silhouettes of officers passed unnoticed on the wall of Alexander's tent. Sergeants shouted, distant horses whinnied and men called for swords but Alexander was still asleep, his arm thrown over his face to block out the sun. Increasingly anxious aides circulated around his door. Eventually, his abashed valet, firmly directed by Ptolemy,* went in and gently shook him. Alexander

---

*A boyhood friend of Alexander's and one of his generals. Later in his career he became Pharaoh of Egypt.

woke at once, apologized to the valet for oversleeping and sprang out of bed to wash his face in cold water. The morning mist had burned off and the day was bright and clear. Alexander put on his white plumed helmet (the better for friend and enemy to find him on the battlefield) and rode out to stand in front of his troops as they formed their line, trumpets sounded and the Persians came thundering to meet them.

After crossing the Ganges, Alexander proclaimed his intention to subjugate India and if there was anything beyond to bend that to his will also and so on to the end of the world. His soldiers, however, had had enough of loot in the sack of Persepolis, enough of hard living in the frozen passes of the Hindu Kush and enough of glory when they dethroned the Emperor Darius. They missed their wives and farms and did not want to die in a strange land where their sons would never tend their graves, and they said that they would go no farther.

Alexander ordered them forward in the peremptory bark they were used to obeying. Then he cajoled them, praised their loyalty and valor, went from man to man and knew each one's name and deeds and wounds, whose life he had saved and who had saved his. Only a little farther, he promised, and then a talent of gold for each of them and all the world would know forevermore what it meant to be a Macedonian. Next he cursed them, called them spiritless curs who were sated with glory after expelling a few hill barons from their mud fortresses—without him they would have been no more than a rabble of cattle thieves. Finally, he said that if all his men were traitors, he would go on alone and at least die with honor, a term with which they were probably unacquainted. He turned his back on them and retired to his tent where he refused both food and entreaty. After three days the men sent emissaries pleading their love, begging him to eat something and keep his strength up so that he, their king, could lead them on the long trip home, and Alexander was at last moved by his veterans' tears.

◆

Alexander's deathbed was in a river-side pavilion within Babylon's high walls. He had been wounded and gone back to the battle line so many times that he had thought he was immortal, but now he knew he was dying. A week ago there had been hope but since then he had faded, although he could still move his head and part of his left arm. His wife Rukshana tended to him, the bloom of her beauty unwilted despite the years with the army under the hard desert sun. Some days his eyes watered with love when she came in to bathe him. Others, he blamed her for his frailty.

Alexander reflected on the contrivance of his legend.

Since he was a boy he had longed to be Achilles, who had never known a moment's doubt or shied away from death even when he knew it was rushing to meet him. Alexander had carefully promoted his identification with the ancient hero, arranging his wars with an eye to the picturesque. The race around the tomb had been planned since the starlit summer night in Athens when he and Hephaestion had decided to invade Persia. He had not slept at all the night before Gaugamela—only through a great exertion of will had he refrained from summoning his generals to go through the battle plan one last time. In the morning he had pretended to oversleep, his arm cast over his face, taking deep, even breaths and occasionally affecting a snore. In India he had been well aware that his supply lines were overextended but had wanted it said that his ambition was limitless, and had pushed his men by inches till he got the gentle mutiny he wanted.

I, he thought, am made of weaker stuff than Achilles and if I am remarkable at all it is for my invention. I have set out to be Achilles and ended up no more than Odysseus of endless contrivance. If I were Achilles I would have died young and at the height of my glory, beloved by all and feared by all, but since I am Odysseus I will suffer an interminable old age and in its good time death will come from the sea.

In that moment Alexander detested his empire, a castle built on sand that he knew would not survive him by a week—already his generals were circling. He wanted to go home to Pella,* linger in the women's quarters, have his mother stroke his hair, hear the laughter echoing in the baths, see the snakes emerge from their shrine to lap up milk with flickering tongues.

With a sense of profound revelation he heard rather than thought the words, "Odysseus returned and so shall I." He saw himself rising up out of bed, lurching toward the door and then striding along the sunlit arcades and alamedas of Babylon, going through the massive lion-carved gates through which ten horsemen could pass abreast, and finally out into the blinding desert where through the grace of the gods, who had often loved and now pitied him, a chariot waited to bear him across the hot sand to the cold sea and a black ship to bear him home.

That evening he lost the use of his voice, and then his hand, and then his eyes, and then he died.

Great strife followed. After several burials his body was disinterred and carried in a golden casket to its final resting place in his most famous city, Egyptian Alexandria, under the eye and reign of Ptolemy.

*The capital of the Macedonian kingdom.

44

LAST ISLANDS

I could not think of myself as old but my world had become a traveler's tale. I thought I should be happy with wealth and lands, son and fame, but I was not, for all that a constant stream of visitors came from far away and thought it a privilege to sit at my table and hear my stories. Though I was approaching my seventieth year I went to the gymnasium daily so that my guests would not wait till I had left and then say, "Can this be the man who was Odysseus?"

Sometimes I wondered if the attention was deserved. In any event the good burghers of Ithaca Town were delighted with my notoriety as it kept the inns full and the market bustling. One of the more enterprising hostelers told me that I should charge my guests an honorarium, a familiarity for which Laertes would have had him flogged, when he was king, but I let it pass.

One day I realized that I had told the stories of the cyclops, the sirens and the duel with Ajax so many times that I no longer remembered the actual events so much as their retellings and the retellings' retellings, which through a gradual accretion of spurious detail and embellishment had, for all I knew, diverged drastically from the truth. Had I really been so beautifully poised while the cyclops glutted himself on my sailors, drawing my sword to kill the beast but checking myself when I realized that victory would mean imprisonment?* Sometimes in dreams my sword-arm went nerveless at the sight of the giant rending and devouring my men and I dropped my blade and scurried behind the monster's cheeses.

I exhumed my old bronze bow from the back of a storeroom. In the torchlight it flickered back and forth between a death-dealing heirloom that had sent countless warriors to Hell and a quotidian implement to hang beside the rakes in a yeoman's cottage. I remembered the battle with the suitors fondly—my once furious resentment had long since faded and each year on the anniversary of the slaughter I sacrificed a ram on the hill where I had dug their grave.

I often wondered what had happened to Pallas Athena. Her absence grieved me and I was no longer sure I had not imagined her. It is unlikely she was an illu-

---

*The cyclops's cave was closed with an enormous stone which only the gigantic cyclops was strong enough to move. Thus, killing him would have meant a slow death by starvation.

sion, I told myself. Most of the details of my travels have become vague but I will never forget the clarity of mind she brought me, like a lucid, sunlit dream.

One night as I sat by the fire with Penelope I told her I was going on a trip to the East, possibly raiding, more likely visiting old friends. I saw her formulate an objection (she would miss me and believed I was more comfortable with her around), conceal it (because she didn't want to be a shrew and thought she'd have a better chance of getting her way indirectly), put on an expression of mild inquiry (to avoid revealing her indirect intentions with a conspicuous blankness) and finally see in my face that I had followed her chain of thought, which made her smile. She told me not to be gone long. I said I would try and I hoped that this time the house would not be full of strange men when I came back. She promised to do her best but could not help the power of her beauty.

I sought out my old companions in their gardens and estates and told them what was in the offing. Many had died (I poured libations of strong wine and honey in the dust before their tombs) and of the living most were infirm, but three of the halest laughed when they heard my plan and said they would like nothing better than to sail with their old captain one more time. They brought out swords that had not been drawn in twenty years and came to port to oversee the lading of the ship.

The odd-job men hanging around the harbor might have smiled to see us greybeards preparing for war but even then there was that in me that kept them civil. We quickly filled out a crew with young men who regretted the strifelessness of the times—they longed to win names and see the world and hoped some of my glory would rub off on them.

It was only as we sailed out of Ithaca harbor that I told them we would retrace my long trip home. Our first port of call was Phaeacia, which we reached in five days of peaceful sailing. We entered the empty harbor at noon. The quiet was profound and we were unsurprised to see the city abandoned. Young trees grew from cracks in the city wall and the rotting remnants of a pier swam below the water's surface. On the quarantine island in the middle of the harbor was a hospital from whose eaves hung beehives, the swarms droning away the afternoon. A herdsman lay in the grass as his cattle drank from a stream gurgling over the beach. When I hailed him he started, gave us a fearful look and hurriedly drove his charges into the woods with great whacks of his stick. The men, eager as hounds, were all for pursuing him but I demurred and we sailed away.

Next was Ogygia, Calypso's island, which seemed to have gotten smaller. I walked spryly enough to the top of the hill where I had passed the days waiting for a ship's sails to nick the horizon (I imagined that it was thirty-five years ago—how it would have felt to look down and see the Ithacan ship bobbing in the cove). I remembered cutting timber for the raft that would bear me away and ran my hands over the axe-scarred pine trunk that had been too thick to fell. I climbed down and went into Calypso's cave with a pang of vanity—she will be as young as when last I saw her, I thought, and for me winter has come, but the low, cool, sand-floored room was empty save for the echoes of the sea. Her bed and loom were gone and the hearth had been effaced—not even a footprint was left. It was peaceful but somehow redolent of weariness, and it felt abandoned. I wondered where she had gone but did not know where to look.

Next was Aiaia, Circe's isle, which had been a thicket then and was a thicket now. Wolf song hung in the evening air and the young men's eyes shone as they hefted their spears. There were signs of recent visitors—cold campfires by the anchorage, piles of smashed pottery, litter in the bushes. I hiked up the hill to Circe's house in the failing light, my men behind with weapons ready.

The walls of her house had burned away, leaving only charred beams, flagstones and the fireplace. Names were crudely carved into the blackened stones, and the noble mantel I remembered, carved with wolves becoming men and men becoming wolves, had been pried out and taken away. Green and gold eyes watched us from the woods but they winked out one by one as the stars emerged, and soon we left.

Next was the island of the cyclops. I expected my men to chafe at venturing onto such dangerous ground but the old companions regarded the prospect with cheerful equanimity and the young men were delighted to finally risk their lives. I stood in the prow with an arrow nocked as we took the ship in toward the familiar beach. "I doubt I could shoot a rook in the heart any-more," I said to my friends, "so it's lucky a cyclops' heart is so big." As we crept up the shingle toward the wood I felt some of the old life come back and I nearly put an arrow into a boy who came running out of the trees. Contrite, I helped him up and dusted him off, and he soon recovered himself; he had seen our ship from the hill and had wanted to be first to greet us; he lived in a house, over the next rise, with his dog, parents and a sister.

He knew little about the cyclopes—they had been gone when the first colonists arrived except for an old blind one who lived alone in his miserable cave and died of unhappiness soon after men came. Where they had gone no one knew, but they had left nothing besides drawings on cave walls and old bones embedded in rock. The boy asked if we had heard of the deeds of great Odysseus, who slew a cyclops in single combat and had the stature of a god? I admitted that I had heard of that Ithacan but did not believe a word of his story and asked to see the bones.

The boy led us to a huge skeleton embedded in a cliff face. The skull had a single wide orbit flanked by fearsome tusks nearly half as long as its body.* Its posture was the record of a death agony. I had meant to go to Polyphemus's cave but found I had no heart for lingering where my men had died so badly, so we went back to the ship and sailed for Troy.

We came within sight of that city in the hour just before sunset when the light falls in warm sheets and makes every face beautiful and every banality poignant. The city walls were higher even than in my memory, with grim silhouettes patrolling and watch fires ablaze on every tower. As the ship coasted into harbor, I had the sudden conviction that my time had come again, that all the ghosts of Troy had come up from Hell to guard their haunted city.

I hefted my spear and was glad of the Trojans in their numbers and the hopelessness of the battle into which we sailed. I felt light and free—this time, I thought, I need no stratagems. The Trojans gave a shout and one of them threw something. I jumped to the side and raised my shield—it took me a moment to realize that the bombardment was not of stones or arrows but the petals of myriad red flowers. As I lowered my shield, the petals clinging to my armor like spattered blood, the cries I had taken for defiance resolved into a chorus of welcome. As

---

*In prehistoric times the Greek islands were home to a number of species of small mastodons. Although they did not long survive the arrival of man, they did leave a fossil record, and, interestingly, their skulls (like the skulls of all pachyderms) have a mono-orbital, cyclopean appearance.

the ship came into the harbor I saw the cheerful crowds on the quay and heard the distant singing.

We berthed between a trading scow and a one-time warship, now gaily painted, its ram sawn off and white bunting strung along its sides. Ashore, vendors sold trinkets and meat cooked on sticks. Children shrieked and parents bought them sweets. My men were delighted— the young ones could barely contain their excitement long enough to tie up the ship before running off to buy tickets, have caricatures drawn, talk to girls, and watch puppet shows—I winced to see a marionette Ajax slaughtering Deineira on a plywood altar amid a welter of fluttering red rags. My old companions took themselves off the ship more gingerly but were pleased to have a stroll in the city that had been the focus of so many years' ambition but which they had never really seen, always having been besieging it or burning it or sailing away.

I walked through Troy jostled by families of every nation. Shops sold drinking cups, gilded statuettes and oddments of armor. There was the square where I had chafed my hands over a fire and drunk the wine of a Trojan patrol, posing as one of them, regaling them with lies. There was a reconstruction of Cassandra's ancient house, though I thought it might be in the wrong street.

Actors worked the crowd, aping famous Greeks and Trojans. I counted four Achilleses, three Hectors, one Patroclus and two each of Priam and Agamemnon. All of them were better-looking than their originals, except for the Achilleses, which I imagined could not be helped. The crowd cleared for a staged combat in which a Hector and a swashbuckling Achilles clacked wooden swords and bellowed insults, often with double entendres. (I remembered Hector and Achilles fighting at dawn in the wasteland between the city and the camp—Hector's focus, discipline and flares of inspiration against Achilles' luminous relentless hatred. They chose the same moment to stop attacking and wait, watching for an opening, the glowing empty space between them vivid in the sudden stillness.) Another actor brushed past me, his face made up in a leer of cruel cunning and an oversized bronze bow in his hand, and after a moment I recognized myself. I watched the actor mount a raised stage to join a handsome actress in a long red wig who wore an expression of beatific sadness while pretending to weave.

As the sun set, I pushed my way through the crowds and out the gates, walking up into the hills from which I could see the city and all its precincts. That was where Agamemnon had his camp, I thought, and that is where Achilles had his funeral games. That ribbon of distant brightness must be the Scamander and that ragged mouth in the old wrecked walls the gate we took the horse through. I said to myself, "Somewhere I must have made a mistake. Turned down the wrong street, opened the wrong door, failed to make a sacrifice when the god was willing. And now I am old and not far from nothing, and everything I knew has turned to smoke."

Something glinted golden in the dust at my feet. I stooped to dig it out and found a disc of metal, a shield. Amazed, I saw that it was made of gold, not only that but it was the very shield forged for Achilles by the divine smith Hephaistos, which I had won at Achilles' funeral games and lost again on the disastrous trip home. It was almost too heavy to lift but I hefted it with both hands and studied its familiar surface. I wondered how it could have come back to Troy—some nereid must have found it in the deep, I reflected, and brought it back to rest near Achilles' tomb.

I could not bear the thought of bringing it back to Ithaca to gather dust on my wall, so in the fading light I walked down to the beach where all our ships had landed so many decades ago and in a sudden access of strength threw it toward the sea. For a moment it seemed to hang motionless in the air and I wondered if my gesture had somehow permitted me to step out of time, but then the shield splashed heavily into the water and the waves closed over it and I went back to my ship with a light heart.

✦

Among the dunes stood Athena, who still watched over him as best she was able. She was relieved to see him sail back toward Ithaca, where, she knew, a peaceful death would find him before the year was out. Like him, the goddess had a light heart. She was grateful that his eyes were not as sharp as they had been and that the light had been flattering but not too bright and he had not noticed that the workmanship of the shield was crude, the figures awkward, that there had been countless other shields just like it for sale cheap among the stalls in Troy's ruins.